LUTA

KEN WILBUR

authorHOUSE®

AuthorHouse™
1663 Liberty Drive
Bloomington, IN 47403
www.authorhouse.com
Phone: 1 (800) 839-8640

Published by AuthorHouse 11/23/2015

ISBN: 978-1-5049-6441-8 (sc)
ISBN: 978-1-5049-6440-1 (e)

ACKNOWLEDGMENTS

I want to thank Rachel Rosenboom, her son Paul and Dale Huggins for allowing me to use their photos in this novel. I also want to thank my son Brent for helping to edit my photos.

I want to thank my sister Ardath and her son Doug for helping to proof read the material.

My granddaughter Kristi Lee Wilbur for coming from the UK to model.

CHAPTER ONE

A muscular eighteen year old, Luta was six feet tall, wiry and a solid one-seventy-five. His chiseled face with high cheekbones showed no sign of a scrub beard. His dark hair was shoulder length and had a healthy shine to it. He sat on his gelding relaxed as he stared into the eyes of an elderly man flanked by half a dozen riders. The man's leathery hands were folded on his saddle horn. His face was deeply wrinkled beneath a thin gray beard. He looked tired, worn out.

"You a hired gun with the cattle barons?" As he spoke his eyes took in Luta. His gray wool shirt, faded blue denim pants and boots that were worn but in good shape. Luta had new heels put on them the last time he was in Denver and they stood out. The pack horse behind Luta was not something a hired gun would have.

"No. I am just riding through." He pushed up the brim of his black, flat-crowned hat so that they could see his dark greenish eyes. He had a Winchester model 1873 in a scabbard under his right leg and a bowie knife in a sheath on his right hip.

"It is dangerous these days to ride through Johnson County, where you headed?"

"Big Bend on Sand Creek."

"What you doing up here in Buffalo?"

"I came from Montana."

"You from the Hole-in-the Wall."

"No. My home is in Eagle Valley a half days ride north of Denver."

"We are experiencing some problems with the cattle barons. They want to keep us off this open range. They call us cattle rustlers and send both the law and their hired guns after us."

"I am neither the law nor a hired gun. I don't have or want a hand in this game."

Luta had never been out of Eagle Valley except to go to Denver or Bear Lake for supplies. He lived with his mother and the man he called Pa. He wanted to see the place where his father had been killed. His mother had told him the story often but he wanted to see it with his own eyes. Luta's father, Big Bear a Cheyenne Chief, had been responsible for many of the raids on the whites.

It was on one of those raids of a wagon train that he captured Luta's mother. They had killed or burned out nearly every homesteader along the South Platte. Freighters refused to make the dangerous trip to Denver. Provisions were scarce, flour sold for forty-five dollars a sack.

Big Bear and Black Kettle were to sign a peace treaty with the commander of Fort Lyon. Big Bear led his band less than forty miles northwest of Fort Lyon where they were told they would be regarded as friendly. Big Bear flew an American flag over his ledge as the Fort Lyon commander had advised him. Meanwhile Col. John Milton Chivington and seven hundred soldiers of the 1st Colorado Cavalry set out for Big Bear's encampment from Fort Morgan. Disregarding the American flag and a white flag that was run up shortly after the soldiers commenced firing howitzers into the camp. After the artillery, the Long Knifes attacked with rifles and swords. Women and children as well as warriors were massacred. But neither Luta nor his mother suffered even a scratch. They were taken to Fort Lyon and then to Fort Morgan where Luta's mother met the man Luta calls Pa.

His mother had taught Luta some of the Cheyenne ways. To give thanks for the joy of living. To give thanks for the morning light, for his health and strength. To give thanks for food, not to kill more game than you need or pick more berries than you will eat. To be kind to the weak, honor the old and give your guest the place of honor in your lodge. To bathe in cold water and once a month to take a sweat bath. She taught him some of the Cheyenne language and never spoke unfavorably of his father or the Cheyenne.

Luta grew up with his white cousins and went to a school taught by his mother. He went to church and learned about Jesus, the miracle of Christmas and Easter. He was much more like his mother and her people than he was his father and the Cheyenne. He learned to work cattle and to hunt. He didn't carry a hand gun as he felt it got in his way but he was a very good shot with his Winchester.

"Better keep a sharp eye if you're riding down toward Casper. There are some that shoot first and ask questions later." He spun his mount and the others followed. They rode back down the grade to the canyon below. Huge red boulders that had tumbled from the rock walls dotted the valley floor. Luta watched until they disappeared behind a row of cottonwood trees.

Luta turned and followed the grassy plateau south. It wound through meadows and sagebrush dropping down to a lake. He found what appeared to be an old camp site of Indians. A circle of rocks they had used to build a fire. He took the pack off Duke, rubbed him down with a handful of grass and put hobbles on him so that he would not wander off. He stripped the saddle off his gelding Lucky rubbed him down and turned him loose. He knew that he would come to his whistle and being loose he would be a better guard. Lucky would let him know if any danger, man or beast approached the camp.

Photo by Dale Huggins

At the water's edge, he striped and entered the water. The water on top was warm but just a few feet below the surface it was cold. This told him that it was spring fed. He didn't swim as much as he washed his body of the trail dust. His last two camp sites had been dry so the lake was a welcome treat. He did not spend much time in the water as he felt uncomfortable being away from his Winchester.

Back on shore, he snapped the dust out of his pants and shirt before putting them back on. He had a clean shirt in his pack but didn't feel it was necessary to change just yet. He tied the red kerchief around his neck. He had worn one for as long as he could remember. His mother said that when he was born his father took one look at him and said, "Luta". In Cheyenne Luta means red or scarlet as he was very red when born. As he did not live with the Cheyenne long enough to earn a Cheyenne name, she just called him Luta. His Pa's name was Kemp Schroeder so he became Luta Schroeder.

He did not look like a half-breed, his hair was dark but not black. His eyes were a dark deep greenish color. He did have high cheek bones but he spoke like a Schroeder not a Cheyenne. He could read, cypher and write which was more than many white men could do. His mother had warned him that as a half-breed he may not be welcome in either the white community or the Cheyenne community.

"Just be yourself Luta, don't let anyone label you and don't you label yourself."

CHAPTER TWO

Mr. Sun was just starting to poke his head up over the ponderosa pines to the east of his camp site. Luta had eaten the bacon he had fried up the night before to get grease to fry the fish he caught. He sat on his haunches enjoying a hot cup of coffee as he watched a crane fish near the shore line. He didn't know its name but this was a nice lake. He felt he was a good twenty miles south of Buffalo.

He could see Duke, his pack horse, grazing down near the lake. He knew Lucky would be around. His thoughts drifted back to the day Lucky got his name. He was a just few days old and had wandered off from his mother. Luta and his Pa were coming to check on the stock when they saw the colt and a big black bear. The bear was about to attack when Luta pulled his Winchester and shot it.

"That's one lucky colt," his Pa said and that became his name. Luta took him when he was weaned and gelded to raise. Each time he would give Lucky grain he would whistle. It was not long before Lucky came running whenever he heard Luta whistle. A great grandson of Blue Eagle he was a deep bluish black and had the same easy riding gait of the Tennessee Walking Stallion.

Making sure the small coffee making fire was out, Luta mounted Lucky and leading Duke rode south around the east side of the lake. It was rolling prairie with some sagebrush and ponderosa pine. The lake turned into a slew, soft and muddy with cattails. He had to swing to the east to stay out of the swampy ground. After a mile or so the slough turned into another lake much like the one where he had camped.

Coming to a road he followed it south around the east side of the lake. It looked to be well traveled, it could be the main road from Casper to Buffalo. He had planned to stay off the roads because if emotions were running high it could be safer. He also wanted to take the trails his father had taken from Montana to Sand Creek at the Big Bend. He knew that a great deal had changed in eighteen years but the lay of the land was the same.

Coming around a bend he saw up ahead a buggy that seemed to have lost a rear wheel. The left side axel was on the ground, the bed of the buggy tilted at an angle. The buggy was loaded heavy with supplies and a woman was unloading it. As he got nearer he could see the woman was really a young girl maybe fifteen or sixteen years old.

She heard him coming and moving to the front of the buggy she grabbed an old double barreled shotgun and pointed it in his direction.

"I mean you no harm." Luta raised his hands shoulder high as he spoke. He continued to walk his horse slowly toward the broken down buggy.

"Just swing out and be on your way." She motioned with the gun for him to swing around to his left.

"I could give you a hand if you like."

"I don't need or want your help, just be on your way."

Luta rode to the side of the broken down buggy keeping his hands up so she could see them. Once there he kicked his left foot out of the stirrup, swung his leg over Lucky and slide to the ground on the right side all the time keeping his hands up and facing her.

"As you can see, I don't have a gun. You can just keep that scatter gun of yours on me and I will see if I can fix your rig." He slowly walked to the back of the buggy with his hands still shoulder height. Bending he looked at the end of the axel and back a few feet to where the wheel had come off.

"I told you I didn't need or want your help."

"I heard you." He walked back to where the wheel was and picked it up. Looking at the track. He leaned the wheel up against the buggy and turned and followed the track back a few hundred feet. He came back to the back of the buggy and finished unloading her supplies.

"I found where the wheel began to wobble but I could not find the nut. The cotter key broke and the nut worked its self-loose. I will go cut a pole to put under the axel so that you can get it home." Without waiting for her to say anything he turned and walked toward a tall ponderosa pine. He found a limb about ten feet long and using his bowie knife cut it off the tree. He put it over the front axle and lifting the buggy he put it under the back axle. It raised the end of the axle up several inches so that it would not dig into the ground. He went to his saddle bag and took out a pigging string to tie the limb in place.

He loaded the supplies back into the buggy and put the wheel on top. "It will get you home and then they can fix it proper." He turned and walked to where Lucky and Duke were grazing.

"Thank you, but I didn't need your help, I could have managed. I am just a couple miles from home. If you will ride ahead of me I would like to pay you with a home cooked lunch." She pointed on down the road to the south.

The road hugged the east side of the lake and coming around a little bend it split, the main road going to the east around a bluff. They stayed near the lake and in a mile or so Luta saw a set of buildings. A log cabin, barn, several corrals and smaller out buildings were nestled up against the bluff. There were several horses in one corral and a couple of milk cows in another. There were chickens and a couple of guinea hens feeding behind the cows. A large dog laying in the shade of the barn came out to meet them, he looked to be part wolf. He didn't bark or wag his tail. He took a position between them and the cabin. The hair on his back standing up.

"It's okay King, go lay down." She pulled the buggy up as near to the cabin as she could. "Tie your horses at the hitch rack." King turned and watched Luta's every move, still not making a sound. Just then the door of the cabin opened and an older lady stepped out.

"Your Pa was beginning to worry, he was about to come see what was holding you up." Just then a man came out of the barn.

"Mom, Dad, this is…." She paused realizing that she didn't know his name.

"Luta, Luta Schroeder." He extended his hand toward the man who was looking at the buggy. They shook hands looking into each other's eyes making an attempt to read what was behind them. Luta turned to the lady on the porch and touched the brim of his hat as he nodded his head.

Turning back to the man, "I looked for the nut but couldn't find it." Luta started to unload the supplies and put them on the porch.

Later riding south Luta thought back at what happened. The mother and father were so thankful that he helped their daughter and she was very flirtatious. That is until she asked about his unusual name and found out that he was half Cheyenne. Than it was as if he had the plague. They could not get him out of their home fast enough. Luta had never experienced anything like this and he didn't understand the emotion he felt. He was more confused than he was angry, more bewildered than he was hurt.

That night by his camp fire he took out his journal and wrote about the day's events. It had been his mother's suggestion, she wanted to read his thoughts as he followed the trail they had taken when he was just a baby. He was still deeply troubled by the change in attitude he encountered. He was having a difficult time putting it on paper when he noticed Lucky standing directly behind him. Lucky had been grazing by a small creek while Luta gathered some things for a salad. He had found some wild asparagus, some golden prairie clover and some cornflower. He also saw some jimson weed and wolfs bane that are quite poisonous.

As he turned to Lucky the gelding gave a soft neigh as if to say, "Are you okay?" Luta found that when he was disturbed, or in pain there were things he could get from the silent devoted companionship of his horse that seemed to make things better. He got up and put his arms around the big black, laying his head on Lucky's neck.

"I am fine. Thanks for your concern. If we have a heavy dew in the morning you stay away from that clover patch, don't want you to bloat." He gave his friend a pat and went back to his journal. The black turned and went to grazing.

The sun was just starting to set in the west when Lucky gave a whinny, he was looking to the south with his ears and head up. Luta reached for his Winchester and laid it across his lap. In just a few seconds he could hear the sound of a shod hoof on rock. He levered a .44-40 caliber round into the chamber. An ounce of prevention was worth a pound of cure.*

"Hello camp!" The voice had an accent that Luta couldn't place. In just a few seconds a man rode out of the ponderosa pine grove, fifty yards south of the camp. He was riding a dun with black mane and tail and leading a roan mule that was loaded heavy.

*Benjamin Franklin is given credit for this but Henry de Bracton, an English jurist said it first in 1268.

"Come on in and step down. Still got some hot coffee if you got a cup but that's all I can offer you, just finished eating everything I fixed." Luta had the muzzle of his Winchester laying on his lap pointed at the horse and rider.

"Coffee sounds good, I got me some jerky and a biscuit." As he dismounted Luta noticed he was rail-thin, about five foot-ten, looked to be middle aged. His cloths hung on him like a scare crow.

He got some jerky and a dry biscuit out of his saddle bag and with a cup in his hand he came to the camp fire. He had a Colt single action Peacemaker on his right hip in an old worn holster that looked to be as old as he was. He held out his cup and Luta poured him a hot cup of coffee. He would take a bite of jerky, dunk his biscuit in the coffee and then take a sip to wash it down.

"Name's Glenn Petersen, going up north to trap me some beaver and pan for gold." He had on an old gray felt hat with the front brim turned up and pinned to the crown with a gold nugget. He saw Luta looking at it. "Fool's gold, thought I had struck it rich but it's just fool's gold. Hope to find some of the real stuff this trip."

His Swedish accent made Luta listen carefully to understand what he was saying.

"I am Luta Schroeder. Headed down to the Big Bend on the Sand River."

"Luta? I have not heard that name."

"It means red in Cheyenne, I was a very red baby and my father called me Luta."

"Cheyenne? You Injun?" Luta could not help but hear the change in his voice, see the change in his manner.

"My father was Big Bear a Cheyenne chief."

"I would never have guessed. You don't look or sound like an Injun." He had finished his jerky and biscuit, he swallowed the last of his coffee and wiped out the cup on his dirty shirt. "Going to have a nice full moon, think I will mosey on up the trail. Want to get these traps in the water as soon as I can. I thank you for the coffee." He backed away from Luta going to where his dun and mule were grazing. He mounted and took off at a trot keeping an eye on his back trail as he hurried north and away from Luta.

CHAPTER THREE

Luta did not need any supplies so he rode around Casper. Casper was located at the foot of Casper Mountain, the north end of the Laramie Mountain Range along the North Platte River. The main road and the railroad both followed the Platte River along the Bozeman Trail. He would ride in the rolling prairie following an old deer or Indian trail south toward Colorado and Sand Creek. Back in 1864 there had been a fort called Platte Bridge Station near where the town now stood. He felt sure with troops there and the mountains to the east, his father and his band would have taken a route much like the one he was riding.

He was still puzzled by the events of yesterday. He never dreamed that people would fear or not want him near them because he was half Cheyenne. Growing up in Eagle Valley he had never seen people have a negative opinion without cause. He had seen how his Pa and the others treated the Indians. He had heard stories of Dull Knife and his band. He knew that the Indians of the plains had killed white settlers and like in his mother's case, kidnapped white women. He knew that they put Indians on reservations but he just never saw himself in that group.

Thinking back at some of the things his mother had said, he now realized she was trying to prepare him for what he was experiencing. She had made an attempt to teach both sides of the Sand Creek massacre. He had learned how the Cheyenne Dog Soldiers after this attack followed up with numerous raids along the South Platte killing many whites, including women and children.

This was years ago, but he was finding out that the opinions of the Indian formed back then, still held true for many whites today. His mother had told him that the Cheyenne could find humor in most everything. He had to smile as he remembered the look on the man's face and his actions last night when he found out that Luta was half Cheyenne.

He was thinking about the very last thing his mother had said to him.

"Just be yourself Luta, don't let anyone label you and don't you label yourself."

He wondered now what she had meant by that. Was she telling him not to allow anyone to label him as a Cheyenne? Was she telling him not to label himself as a Cheyenne? She had told him to just be his self. But isn't that what he had been doing? He had been honest and his honesty had made people fear and distrust him.

Those people had no cause to fear or distrust him and they didn't until he told them how he got his name. He wondered how things would have been different if he hadn't told them he was Luta Schroeder. He smiled when he remembered what little Squirt called him. She couldn't say Luta when they were both learning to walk and talk so she just called him Lou.

She did not come out to wave or say goodbye. She could not understand why he felt it was necessary to take this trip. His mother had taught them all about Sand Creek, what more could he learn by following the route of a band of Indians. Squirt, her given name was Martha after her grandmother Wilbur. She was his best friend. They did everything together, hunting, fishing, and working the cattle and horses. When they were little she had even talked him into playing house. He remembered how he hated it until the day she gave him a kiss when he came into their make believe house. She had explained that was what married people do.

He was still thinking about Squirt and hoping that she had got over being angry with him, when he saw a thin wisp of smoke up ahead. He could tell by the smoke that it was a small fire. There was not even a hint of a breeze so the smoke was going straight up. As he topped a small ridge he heard a calf bawl. Riding around a large boulder he saw a clearing and two cowboys who had just released a calf they had branded.

They were busy kicking dirt on the fire and didn't notice him until he was well into the clearing. He watched the calf hurry to its mother and noticed that the brand on the old cow matched the brand on the calf.

The cow and calf worked their way into the brush to where several other cows with calves grazed. He was walking toward the two cowhands when he noticed a coiled copperhead about to strike the calf, they had disturbed him sunning on a rock and he was in a foul mood. Luta pulled his Winchester and remembering that he had a round in the chamber thumbed back the hammer and snapped off a shot. The cowboys turned to see the head of the rattler separate from its body and fly into the brush. Duke jumped a little but Lucky didn't even seem to notice he had taken a shot. Leaving the empty under the hammer for safety, Luta returned his Winchester to its scabbard.

"That's a real steady horse, that's not the first time he has been shot over." Both men had their hands on the colts on their hips but neither drew their weapon. The one doing the talking was about his age, a little on the chubby side and had several days' growth that was still working on being a beard. It was sandy in color and patchy.

"No, I have hunted off him for a couple years." Luta was now ten to twelve feet from them and Lucky stopped on his own. The other hand was taller, he seemed to have nervous eyes that darted from Luta to his pard. He was wearing old cavalry breeches and a blue flannel shirt. He was older by several years.

"What you hunt?" Luta knew it was his way of asking if he was a lawman, a bounty hunter or a hired gun.

"Deer and bear. When the bear come out of hibernation they are real hungry and that is about the same time the cows are dropping calves." Luta noticed the brand on their two cow ponies was the same as that on the cow and calf. This told him they were a couple hands working for that brand.

"You doing some hunting here in Wyoming?"

"No. Just riding through. An older gent up near Boulder asked me that same question a couple days ago." Luta had his hands folded on the saddle horn, reins between his fingers. "He told me emotions were riding high and to be on the lookout. But I thought once I was passed Casper the trouble was behind me."

"Seems to be trouble all over the Wyoming Territory these days. With cattle prices getting higher rustling is increasing. We got us a chuck wagon and camp a couple miles to the south, you interested in some beans you are welcome to ride in with us." They turned and went to their horses that were ground reined, mounted and followed the deer trail south.

Their camp was next to an artesian well, water gushing from it formed a pond several feet deep with the over flow going back underground. A few big cottonwoods gave them shade from the afternoon sun. They had a remuda where the hands could select their mounts for the day. It was evident that they had been camped here for several days.

The hand who had been doing the talking gave his horse to the other man and walked to the chuck wagon. He was talking with an older man and the cook. Luta did not want to stare but out of the corner of his eye he could see him pointing and make gestures as he talked. Luta tied Duke and Lucky to a rope strung between two cottonwoods. He loosened the latigo so that Lucky could breathe easier. He would let them cool down in the shade before letting them drink.

"This is our top kick, Hank Helmers, I didn't catch your name."

"Lou Schroeder." Luta held out his hand and felt the callous of many years of cowboying. The foreman's steel gray eyes were on Lucky more than Luta. Over the years he had learned to judge a man by his horse more then by the clothes he wore.

"Nice gelding. What's his blood line?"

"Tennessee Walking Horse and mustang cross. He is about three-fourths Tennessee and a quarter mustang."

"You raise em?"

"Yes, about a half days ride north of Denver. My Pa and his brother-in-law have a horse and cattle spread."

"What you doing in the Wyoming Territory?"

"Just stretching my legs. I have spent all my life in the valley and I just wanted to see some of the country."

"Chub tells me you are better than average with that Winchester."

"I guess maybe I am, I grew up with it and most always hit what I aim at."

"Where you headed from here?"

"South, to Colorado and then back home." Luta didn't like to lie but he had to admit it was working better than telling the truth.

"Cookie has some sourdough bullets, chuck wagon chicken and Pecos strawberries, if you want to get yourself a plate." The foreman turned and walked over to have a closer look at Lucky. Good horseflesh was always of interest to a cowboy.

Luta went to the chuck wagon and got a tin plate of biscuits, bacon and beans. This was a staple cowboy menu from Texas to Montana.

CHAPTER FOUR

Luta passed up their offer to help with the round-up. The more he saw of the land, the better he liked the valley. He missed Squirt and wondered if she was still angry. He was writing this in his journal without even thinking. He also wrote that the people seemed to like Lou Schroeder better than they did Luta Schroeder. He smiled thinking it was the same guy but it was just how the people perceived him.

He had rode that day over land, rising and falling like ocean swells of buffalo grass, sage and prickly pear. He kept the Laramie Mountains off to the east and Elk Mountain to the west. He was camped on a bluff overlooking a river which he did not know the name of. He had camped down by the water and let the horses graze as he washed up and ate his supper. After cleaning up his dishes he felt the need to move, so he packed up and climbed to the bluff where he camped.

He felt it was still a good day's ride south to the Colorado border. He had stopped at a trading post at Rock River for a few supplies early in the afternoon and the man told him he was northwest of Laramie. He had rode cross country keeping the main road to Laramie well to the east. He wondered how different it had been in the fall of 1864. A band of two hundred Cheyenne men, women and children following the restless winds of the prairie. Luta could not picture in his mind what it must have been like to lead them.

He thought about how different his life would have been without the Sand Creek massacre. He would have grown up as a Cheyenne, never knowing Eagle Valley or Squirt. He would not have gone to school, most likely would not speak English and would not know the ways of the white man. He wondered about his father Big Bear. He went to sleep thinking about all the details his mother had told him and all that he had read on the Sand Creek Massacre.

Big Bear and his band were to meet up with Black Kettle, leading a band of Southern Cheyenne and a band of Arapahos under Chief Niwot. In accordance with a peace parley they were to relocate to Big Sand Creek where they were guaranteed safety. Black Kettle flew an American flag with a white flag beneath it over his lodge as advised.

Meanwhile, U.S. Army Colonel John Chivington, a Methodist preacher, freemason and opponent of slavery and his seven hundred soldiers of the 1st Colorado Cavalry and a company of the 1st Regiment New Mexico Volunteer Cavalry set out for the encampment from Fort Morgan.

"Damn any man who sympathizes with Indians! ... I have come to kill Indians, and believe it is right and honorable to use any means under God's heaven to kill Indians. ... Kill and scalp all, big and little; nits make lice."—- Col. John Milton Chivington

Chivington had the howitzers loaded with canister and began to fire on the encampment. It should be noted that Chivington did not command disciplined troops. They were not well-trained and for the most part were boisterous, vengeful, independents from the wild mining camps. Hundreds of Cheyenne men, women and children were slaughtered and their corpses mutilated in the massacre. The soldiers fired on them through the afternoon, firing more than a ton of bullets and cannonballs. Sand Creek ran red with Cheyenne and Arapaho blood. They burned the village and killed the wounded. Indian women hide their babies inside hollow trees and logs. They would dig a hole in the sandy bank of the creek and hide. But Cheyenne and Arapaho blood soaked the ground of Big Sand Creek.

Big Sand Creek meanders like a rattlesnake through the tall buffalo grass and this helped to save a few. Most of the deaths were caused by the cannonballs. Canister shot consists of a cylinder filled with round balls of lead or iron.

photo by Rachel Rosenboom

CHAPTER FIVE

Luta woke up to a morning of rain and fog. Lucky and Duke were immune to poor weather and he would have to adjust rather than try to fight Mother Nature. He dug his rain slicker out of his pack, it was black canvas and came down to his knees. The slicker had been treated with oils and beeswax to provide waterproofing. It had metal buttons and a corduroy collar and when he was mounted it covered the saddle, giving him a dry seat. He didn't take time to fix coffee or breakfast, he would chew on some jerky once packed up and headed south. There was no breeze and the fog was so thick he would be wet to the bone without the slicker. Dense fog presented a hazard for them.

He just let Lucky pick his way and pace. In places the footing was not good. Lucky and Duke were shod and their shoes were in good shape so once they were down off the bluff and on the deer trail they made better time. The visibility down by the river was considerably better than up on the bluff but it was still not more than fifty or sixty feet.

There was no sign of Mr. Sun and Luta had no clue what time it was. He had planned to get him a pocket watch. Wade had told him the best place to get one was a train station. The telegraph operator would have a good stem wind watch for sale at a good price. He shouldn't have to pay more than a dollar for a nice nickel plated time piece. The problem was, he had not been anywhere near a train station and unless he changed his route, he wouldn't come near the railroad.

The deer trail followed the river and if his sense of direction was correct, they were going south. After several hours they came to a bend in the river. High flood water and erosion in the sandy rock had made an overhang and what looked like a cave. It looked like a good place to build a fire and wait for Mr. Sun to burn off the fog.

Luta found some drift wood up against the back wall that was dry so he made a small coffee making fire. The overhang was large enough for him and the two horses to get in so he striped them and gave them each a little grain that he carried for times like this when they couldn't graze. The fog was still so thick that he could just see the west bank of the river which was maybe sixty feet. He got out his journal and with a hot cup of coffee in one hand and a stub of a pencil in the other, he wrote a few observations.

He decided to try his luck fishing, he had always heard that if there was a mist of rain the fish would bite very well. He took a small bit of a biscuit and baited his hook. He would toss it up stream and let it float down over what appeared to be a deep hole. After fifteen or twenty minutes and several bits of biscuit he looked around for some better bait. Under a rock he found a grub worm. About the third toss he got a strike, setting the hook he felt that it was a good sized fish. After a short fight, he managed to drag the fish up on shore. It was a nice sized bass, maybe two pounds. Large enough to make a good supper.

Night came with a blackness Luta had rarely seen. The fog hid the stars and moon, the light from his camp fire reflected off the sand stone wall but toward the river it was as if a very large black blanket covered the world. He watched the flickering flame and remembered hearing that you could see Indian Chiefs in the flame if you stared hard enough. He didn't know about that, but he did know that if you looked into the flame and your eyes adjusted to it, you couldn't see anything when you looked away. Tonight it didn't matter that much as you couldn't see your hand in front of your face if you were out of the circle of light from the small camp fire.

He got the coffee pot ready to put on the fire in the morning, rolled out his bed and using his saddle as a pillow he closed his eyes wondering what the morning would bring. He had been on the trail for less than two weeks and he had learned that he preferred life in the valley. He seemed to be thinking of Squirt more and more. Wondering what she was doing, if she missed him as much as he missed her. Was she still angry? He knew how she could pout, sulk if she didn't get her way which seldom happened as she could be very persistent.

The next morning it was a different world. Mr. Sun was up and doing his thing, the fog had lifted, the clouds had disappeared and the sky was a clear blue. Everything looked and smelled so fresh and clean. Luta couldn't help but sit in the saddle a little straighter showing pleasure and satisfaction with the start of this new day.

"I think I must get my energy from the sun Lucky, I feel so much better today than I did yesterday." Lucky's ears perked up at the sound of his master's voice. The big gelding really enjoyed the companionship of this human. Horses tend to view humans as predators and their survival depended on their ability to flee. Lucky seemed to understand that this humans survival often depended upon him and he was always there for him. Duke was not so loyal, without the hobbles he would run off at night.

Lucky would communicate with Luta in various ways. Nickering, squealing, or whinnying and nuzzling along with his body language. A combination of ear position, neck and head height, foot stomping or a whinny would alert Luta to possible danger. Lucky had four basic vocalizations, his neigh or whinny, his nicker, the squeal and snort. These sounds along with ear position allowed Luta to interpret a message from Lucky. When he stomped his foot he was expressing discomfort, irritation, impatience or anxiety. With his head and neck up, he was alert and often tense, a lowered head and neck was a sign of relaxation.

Horses are creatures of habit and have excellent memory. They also have a strong social bond, this can be a bond for their herd or for a human. Being a large animal and retaining some wild instincts they can react with biting, striking or kicking. Lucky had trust and confidence in Luta but he could act greatly different toward a stranger who made an attempt to control him.

Luta noticed Lucky was walking with one ear forward the other backward, with his head down. This told him that Lucky was relaxed but wanting to hear anything that could be coming up behind them or ahead of them. The interaction they enjoyed was a comfort to both of them. With Lucky on the alert Luta could enjoy the lush meadows, waterfalls, and canyons. He would often spot some Bighorn sheep, Mule Deer, or Bison.

Before the railroads and Buffalo hunters, there were massive herds of buffalo or American Bison. Now Luta would see these magnificent beasts only occasionally in small herds grazing on sweeping native grasses in the meadows or canyons. Their daily routine was grazing, resting and cud chewing. Then moving to a new location to graze again. Luta was seeing more elk, moose and mule deer than buffalo.

Photo by Rachel Rosenboom

The moose were rarely in groups, but mating season was coming so he would see them in close proximity to one another. The males would make loud grunting sounds that could be heard as far as five hundred yards. The females produce a wail-like sound. The elk also have a language all their own. A bull growling for a female may throw in a challenge bugle to another bull. Elk talk year round and bulls often make the same sounds cows do. Calves, cows and bulls all have their way of calling to other elk.

It could be very noisy out on the prairie. Throw in the cry of a bobcat, the howl of wolves or coyotes, the screech of an owl, the warning barking of prairie dogs or the deep hooting moan of the prairie-chicken and you could have a chorus that would frighten even the bravest.

Lucky had heard a different sound, Luta noticed his ears go forward and his head come up. Luta now heard this new sound. Topping a knoll Luta saw a sea of baaing sheep. The sheepherder and his dog were in the center of the flock near a covered wagon. He had hitched a team of mules to the wagon and was climbing up to the seat.

The grass was exhausted in the area, it appeared the herder was moving his bleating flock to better grass. Luta pulled up Lucky and watched from the knoll. The herder took the wagon out ahead of the flock and the dog followed behind the flock, pushing the stragglers along by nipping at their heels. If one would break for the open the dog would run and grab it by the ear and drag it back to the group. Luta thought there must be near two thousand making a steady baa, baa as the slowly moving mass followed the wagon.

Luta noticed the grass in the area had been eaten to the ground. It would take months of good rain before anything could graze on this range. Luta could see why there was a mutual hatred between cattlemen and sheep men. This was open range but the sheep ruined it for the cattle or the elk, deer, and moose. The reason for this is that ruminant animals, those that chew a cud, do not have upper incisors. They pull their heads back when taking a bite of grass and for this reason do not eat it so short. The sheep, horse and deer eat it shorter because they have upper incisors, they tend to pinch it off at ground level. He remembered his Pa explaining this to him when they were moving the mares with foals to another area of the valley.

Luta followed at a distance watching the dog work the sheep and remembering his dog. He and Denver were together all the time. Denver sleep at the foot of his bed and was never more than a few steps from him. Judith, Squirt's mother, wouldn't allow Denver in their house so he waited on the porch. The same on Sunday when they went to church, he would wait at the door for Luta. If Luta and Squirt went for a ride, Denver was always with them. A tear came to his eye when he thought how Denver had to struggle to keep up as he got older. Saying goodbye to his faithful friend was the most difficult thing he has ever had to do.

The herder led the flock to a small creek where they spread out and drank their fill. Luta was following them watching the sea of wool line the creek bank. He was thinking how difficult and lonely the life of a sheepherder must be. He was entrusted with a large investment that he and his dog had to watch twenty-four hours a day. It was not a job that you could give to a lazy or unreliable man.

Luta saw one of the sheep keel over suddenly, and then another. Now he heard the report of the rifles. Looking to his right across the creek he saw three riders with their rifles to their shoulders. He touched Lucky with the heel of his right boot and Lucky jumped into a lope down a draw toward the three gunmen. In just seconds he was coming out behind some brush a hundred yards from the riders. Pulling Lucky to a halt he drew his Winchester.

He did not know the reason for the shooting but it was not a fair fight and the herder was too far away to help his sheep. Luta levered a cartridge into the chamber and adjusted the graduated rear sight. He did not want to shoot to kill or even injure them but he wanted to stop the shooting of the sheep. He took careful aim at the saddle horn of the rider who appeared to be the leader of the group. He squeezed off a shot and leather from the top of the horn seemed to take flight. When they heard the sound of the report they lost their appetite for shooting defenseless sheep, wheeled their horses and disappeared over the ridge.

CHAPTER SIX

Javier Herrera a slight, short but wiry man with dark skin, made darker by years working in the sun, was about Luta's age. He worked for the Two Bar, a large outfit owned in part by the Warren family. It had been a cattle only ranch but they added sheep much to the displeasure of some of their neighbors in the cattle business. It appeared that even this giant ranch was not immune from sheep raiders.

Luta could understand why the cattlemen did not want sheep on the open range, he had seen the bare, weed less, grassless, and flowerless swath they destroyed as they grazed. But on the other hand it was open range and the sheep had as much right to it as the cattle.

Javier had cut some steaks off one of the dead ewe, opened a can of beans and with some day old biscuits they were eating supper. Luta preferred beef, deer or even bear to the mutton but he was making the best of it. He did want to move on before dark as he did not want to spend a night with the sheep.

"Thank you for the grub Javier, I think I will amble on a ways before dark sets in." Luta was finishing his second cup of coffee.

"Thank you for your help, your excellent shot surprised me as much as it did the raiders."

"You said we are almost on the Colorado border?" They had been talking earlier about the lay of the land.

"Yes, you will cross the border to Colorado and then the South Platte River just a few miles south of here."

Luta wanted to get on the other side of the river before making camp in the Platte valley. His journey was proving to be more educational than he had anticipated it would be. He was learning that his life in the valley had been sheltered from many of the trials and tribulations others faced daily.

Luta wanted to visit two locations and he was getting near both of them. He wanted to see the spot where his grandfather was ambushed and his mother captured. His mother had told him that Big Bear said only her beauty saved her from the fate of the others. At Sand Creek the tables were turned and it was Big Bear and many of his people that were slaughtered.

In both cases, his mother had survived. He had often over the years asked her how she managed to carry on after her father was killed. She told him that as a small girl her father had taught her the game of poker and had instilled in her the belief that poker was much like the game of life. You had to play the hand that you were dealt but that not always did the person with the best hand win the pot. Often one player could run a bluff and get the other to fold. It wasn't always what you held in your hand but what the other player or players thought you held. Yes, she had struggled to understand why she was saved and felt that maybe it was to be his mother. To raise him to be a good man.

Luta had asked her what it was like living with the Cheyenne and she had simply told him that working and living like an Indian woman for a year was enough to last her a life-time.

She had told him that things could have been very different. That her father and his wagon train were only a couple days from Denver. Because of all the Indian raids and the demand for supplies at the mining camps the cost of goods had more than doubled. When he sold his goods he would have enough money to have the ranch he had always dreamed about. He would sit by the camp fire in the evenings with a cup of coffee and tell her of their ranch.

This valley and the ranch that your Pa and I have is what your grandfather dreamed. The rich grass and the clear blue spring fed streams. He wanted to sit on his porch and watch his horses and cattle grazing. Grass and water were absolutely necessary for his dream to come true. Just a few days and he would have had significant profit to pay for his dream.

Coming to the Platte, Luta thought how fickle life could be. It could change without reason. Had his grandfather's dream come true, there would be no Luta. What side of this was he on? Was he glad that Big Bear had killed his grandfather and captured his mother? Was he glad that Chrivington and his soldiers had killed Big Bear? This had not been so complicated when he rode out of the valley. He had this adventure in his mind to travel the same route the Cheyenne took to Sand Creek. To somehow experience a little of their life on the trail was like.

It was not working out the way he had planned. People were not the same as those in the valley. They were not like those he encountered when getting supplies in Denver or Big Bear.

He now realized it was a minor miracle that he was alive today.

Watching the flickering flame of his coffee fire he couldn't make up his mind what he wanted to do. It no longer seemed important to see Sand Creek or the spot where his grandfather was ambushed. It just dawned on him how he was the product of two very bad battles. He was alive because in both cases the victor had committed a massacre.

Just being alive was only the start. He was who he was today because of people he took for granted. His Pa. Luta realized that Kemp loved his mother and because of his love for her he accepted him. But he had always treated him like a son, not like some other man's son. Even now when Kemp had a daughter of his own, he did not feel like she was held in higher esteem than he was.

He was just beginning to realize that having a happy home was more than just a roof over his head, it was a foundation for all that he was. Kemp and his mother had not only told him how to live but they showed him how to live. He couldn't do anything about the past but he could do something about the future. His future wasn't at Sand Creek, or on the Overland Trail where his grandfather died, his future was where he started from.

CHAPTER SEVEN

"Squirt, I am tired of all this. You mope around all gloomy and sad. What's done is done. Get over it."

"But what if I never see him again? I didn't even say good-bye." She was getting her horse saddled to ride down to the gate again. She was hoping to see Luta riding in, to meet him.

"He will get here, if and when he gets here. You acting like this is not going to help." Her dad was mucking out the horse stall. He had never seen this side of his daughter. She was always so strong, so positive."

"It has been over three weeks, he should have been back by now." She pulled the latigo tight and dropped the stirrup so she could mount. With her left toe in the stirrup and her left hand with the reins on the horn she swung into the saddle. When she hit the seat, her horses head and ears came up, her mare was ready to run. She leaned forward, ducking her head as she rode out of the barn.

Walking to the cabin Wade watched his baby girl, who was becoming a young woman, ride toward the morning sun.

"You have to do something about that daughter of yours." Wade took the cup of coffee Judith handed him and took a seat at the table.

"Oh, when she is depressed she is my daughter and when she is happy and perky, she is daddy's girl."

"You said it, but yes, that sounds about correct." Wade sipped his coffee he wished like most fathers he had some magic words to make his little girl feel better.

"I am about ready to send her to Bear Lake to help Sarah and Dusty. Get her out of the house, out of the valley for a while." Judith poured herself a cup of coffee and took a seat across the table from Wade. "Carmen said she was over there yesterday trying to talk Chet into going and looking for Luta."

"Chet won't be leaving Carmen when she is expecting their baby any day. Guess she knows better than to ask me. If she goes to Bear Lake you think she will bug Dusty?"

"Her sister is not going to let Dusty run off on a wild goose chase, so I think Martha knows better than to ask." Judith opened the Big Bear cookie jar and offered Wade an oatmeal cookie to go with his coffee.

"How do you plan to get her to go to Bear Lake?" He took a cookie and dunked it in his coffee.

"I will just tell her that I think Luta will go to Bear Lake before he comes here as it is on his way. I don't think she should ride to Bear Lake alone, too many shady characters on the road these days."

"I agree. If Kemp doesn't need any supplies, I will go with her. I talked to Kemp and Pat, they too are worried about Luta but they both think that it was necessary for him to get this out of his system."

"I have faith in Luta. He is strong and he has a good head on his shoulders. But we both know that things can happen out of his control. How long do we wait before we do send out a hunting party?"

"Kemp and I feel with normal traveling he should be at Sand Creek by now. That is still several days ride east of here. We thought that if we didn't see any sign of him in a week we would ride toward Sand Creek, see if we could cross his path. With his big black and pack horse people will tend to remember if they see him."

"You do know that if your daughter knows you are going you will have to either hog tie her or take her with you."

"That is why I liked your idea of sending her to Bear Lake, we could get away without her knowing it. I am hoping that Luta shows up before that time."

"You think Luta is missing her as much as she misses him?" Judith got up from the table and went to the kitchen window. She remembered the many times she stood waiting for Wade to ride up. She remembered the empty feeling she had when Wade was gone. She needed to be more understanding of her daughter, when an important person in your life is missing, the whole world seems empty.

"I don't know. I know that he has feelings for her, that he has always allowed her to make decisions on what they would do. That is why I was a little surprised when he went against her strong objections this time." Wade got up and went to Judith, standing behind her with his arms around her waist, his chin on the top of her head. "Sweeny and I are going to move some of the cows and calves, could be a little late for lunch." He gave her a little pat on her rump and started for the door.

"Aren't we just Mr. Romantic?"

CHAPTER EIGHT

Luta had not slept well, he had not been able to turn his mind off. His thoughts bounced back and forth between the massacre of Sand Creek, the attack on his grandfather's wagon train and his home in the valley. He would get a vision of Indians being slaughtered and then of Indians slaughtering white men. He would see the trout stream in the valley and then it would turn into Sand Creek red with Cheyenne blood. He woke up in a sweat in the middle of the night. His coffee fire had burned out but the smell of the pine smoke was still in the air.

He laid on his back looking at the Milky Way high overhead. He liked to gaze into the night sky. Find the North Star and the Big Dipper. Tonight the stars and constellations were so bright, it was almost like he could reach out and touch them.

He was about to turn on his side and close his eyes when he heard a horse shoe strike a rock. He didn't think it was Duke or Lucky as it was too distant, he didn't think they would be that far away. Just as he was sitting up to listen, Lucky gave him a warning nicker. He reached for his boots, turned them upside down and shook them to make sure nothing had crawled in and then pulled them on. His hand found his Winchester as he got to his feet.

He heard it again, it was still several hundred yards away. He gave Lucky a soft whistle and the big gelding came to him. He did not know where Duke was, but thought he was behind him. The sound of shod hoofs was now mixed with the occasional squeak of saddle leather, the jingle of a spur, and the sound of unshod hoofs. The sounds grew nearer and nearer until Luta could see some moving shapes. They were following the creek bank and would pass between him and the creek. He could now make out three riders pushing twelve to fifteen head of cattle ahead of them. Moving cattle at this time of the night could mean only one thing. Rustlers.

His fire had long since died out and he was up against a dark bank, under a large ponderosa pine so he felt confident that they would not see him. He did not want to encounter them. If they were surprised they would most likely shoot first and ask questions later. He did not want to get shot or to have to shoot anyone. The first of the cattle were now passing. One of the riders was riding on the flank to keep them bunched and he would pass twenty-five to thirty feet from Luta and Lucky. He was watching the cows so his eyes would not be toward Luta and Lucky.

They were moving at a good steady pace but it seemed like it took ages for them to pass. Luta's palms were sweaty holding the Winchester. They were now moving out of sight and Luta took a big sigh of relief. He gave Lucky a pat and removed his boots to crawl back in his bedroll. This time sleep came rather quickly. He slept deep and hard until Mr. Sun poked his head up over the eastern horizon.

He was just buckling the last strap on Duke when he heard some riders coming. He turned and pulled the Winchester from the scabbard on Lucky waiting for them to come into the open.

"Morning, just poured out the last of my coffee to make sure the fire was out." At the sound of his voice the three rider's heads snapped in his direction as if they were one. They had all been riding with their heads down reading the sign.

"You see those rider's and cows come through here?" A wiry middle aged man with a bony face, birdlike eyes and a narrow nose appeared to be the leader of the group. But it was a pudgy younger rider with shaggy dark hair and round face that held Luta's attention. He looked angry.

"Yeah, they passed here in the middle of the night, four or maybe five hours ago." Luta kept Duke between him and the riders.

"Rustled some of our stock." He took the makings out of his shirt pocket and rolled a smoke. The angry young rider had a dead cheroot clenched in his teeth. The third rider had long strawberry blond hair down to his shoulders and didn't appear to be more than fifteen.

"Figured as much, honest men don't move cattle in the middle of the night."

Luta pulled the canvas cover down over the pack on Duke, checked the cinch to make sure it was snug and casually moved to the head of Lucky. He still carried his Winchester in his right hand.

"You doing some prospecting?"

"No, just riding through, on my way home."

"Where's home?"

"Half days ride north of Denver." Luta now checked the girth of Lucky's, put his toe in the stirrup and swung into the saddle. When he mounted with his Winchester in his right hand, it came into view, pointed in their direction. He put the barrel in the scabbard on his saddle and pushed it down into place all in one motion.

Seeing the Winchester for the first time made all three riders stiffen to attention. Seeing Luta push the rifle into the scabbard, they relaxed. They now knew that he had been prepared and after the exchange of conversation, they knew he felt he had nothing to fear. Body language could be so important, it often said more than the spoken word.

How you are perceived, how and what others think of you is so important. The law was a long way away so you had to be strong, able to take care of yourself and protect your property. Luta did not look down and out, he did look able to respond if necessary. In any case, these men were looking for the men who had rustled their cattle, they were not looking for or wanting any trouble.

They turned and followed the tracks of the cattle and Luta followed their back trail. Both had learned something. They now knew about how far behind the rustlers they were and Luta learned that he would most likely come upon a ranch before long.

CHAPTER NINE

"That young cowhand from the circle C has been in here the last three days."

"Yes, think he has an eye for my little sister."

"Is she encouraging him?"

"No, she just has to be herself."

"Well at least when she is helping a customer she has a smile on her face and in her voice. When your dad dropped her off she looked and acted like she had come from a funeral."

Dusty and Sarah were watching Squirt help a young man pick out a shirt. It was his second new shirt in as many days. They were glad to have the extra help, there was always something to do, someone to wait on at their outpost. When they started this adventure a year ago they wondered if their only customers would be those living in the valley. Bear Lake was growing, it now had a post office and would soon have a bank. Their outpost was now a general store in a growing community.

"This one brings out the blue in your eyes." Squirt was holding up a blue flannel shirt in front of the cowboy.

"Okay, I will take this one."

"Will there be anything else for you today?"

"Well....there is this BBQ and square dance Saturday night. I was wondering if you would like to go?"

"Oh, thanks but I don't know if I will still be here. If I am and if my sister and her husband go, I will go with them and we can have a dance." She was taking the shirt to the cash drawer. "That will be fifty cents."

The nervous cowboy gave her the money and hurried out to his horse at the hitch rack. He was encouraged by the thought of a dance. The next few days could not go fast enough. He would be at the dance wearing one of his new shirts and clean pants.

The smell of the hickory smoke and the ribs drifted over the crowd which were forming for the BBQ and square dance. Dusty watched as one of the cooks put a large honey conb into one of the big black bean pots. The honey with the side pork would make those beans extra tasty.

Later Dusty, Sarah and Squirt were at one of the picnic tables enjoying ribs, beans and corn bread. People were still coming. They were going to have a large crowd. After their toil of life these settlers, ranchers and pioneers felt a need for an activity that would provide recreation as well as social contact with neighbors. The BBQ and square dance filled this need.

Some of the ranchers and settlers were at odds over land and water rights but they tended to call a truce for these times. This social was sponsored by the church and the pastor had asked them to be thankful for this opportunity to join in fellowship he said the grace.

"There's that cowhand and he is wearing one of the new shirts I sold him."

"That is not just a cowhand, that is Jesse Collins the son of old man Collins who owns the circle C ranch." Dusty was wiping his plate with the last of his corn bread and thinking about going back for another helping.

"Dusty, I can tell you are thinking about going back for seconds. If you do, you will be too full to dance." Sarah put her hand on his arm. "I will take our plates and silverware and put them in the basket."

The band was beginning to tune up on the stage

(a hay rack) one of the ranchers had donated for the night. Bear Lake did not have a hall big enough to hold this crowd. That was what the church hoped to build with the collection they would take and the donations people had given going through the food line.

The band would have two fiddles, a banjo and a washtub bass or gutbucket that had a single string. The player would adjust the pitch by pulling or pushing on a staff to change the tension of the string. The tighter the tension the higher the pitch. In this group the player of the washtub was also the caller.

The caller would sing out directions to the beat of the music. A square was four couples facing each other in the form of a square. Promenade, swing your partner, do-si-do, allemande left or right. All these told the couples what to do. It was as much fun watching as it was to dance.

They would mix in a Virginia reel from time to time where five to seven couples would line up facing their partners and do dancing moves to the beat of the music.

It was the very first Virginia reel that Jesse came and asked Squirt to dance. It was the young couples turn to show their dancing ability. Many of the young had not mastered the square dancing routine but they all knew the Virginia reel.

Jesse was proud as a peacock. His partner was the prettiest girl in the line. Most had never even seen her before so she drew the most looks and the greatest interest. The caller sang out the moves to the young dancers as they moved to the beat of the music.

After the dance, Jesse escorted Squirt back to where Dusty and Sarah were seated. "This is my sister, Sarah and her husband Dusty....I am sorry but what is your name?" Squirt didn't want him to know that she knew who and what he was.

"We know Jesse." Dusty said with a big smile.

"Thank you....for the dance....and your name is?"

"Martha, Martha Wilbur. And you are welcome, I enjoyed it." Sarah and Dusty were grinning from ear to ear. They were enjoying the exchange between these two young people. After Jesse had gone Dusty looked at Martha and asked.

"Martha is it, and what happened to Squirt?"

CHAPTER TEN

Photo by Ken Wilbur

Luta had been riding for several hours when he came upon a paint mare. She wasn't wearing a halter but he knew at first glance she was not a wild horse. At closer inspection he could see that she was shod. Nice conformation, the paint mare showed a good blood line.

When the mare saw Luta she turned and started walking in the direction Luta was going, so he followed. She came upon a deer trail and took it. She looked back over her shoulder from time to time to make sure Luta was still there.

"Where do you think you're going with my mare?" The woman's voice came from a ridge. Luta turned to see a woman and two men looking down on him.

"I don't know if your mare is leading me or if I am pushing her." Luta pulled Lucky up and folded his hands over the saddle horn. "Came up on her a couple miles back, she found this deer trail and we followed."

"Patty got run off last night when somebody stole a dozen or so of our cows." She was an attractive, pale skinned brunette, flanked by a large man with a neatly trimmed goatee and a bronze-faced chubby-cheeked man wearing a tall ten-gallon grey felt hat.

"Early this morning I talked to three hands trailing some stolen cows. They were about five hours behind the rustlers."

"Was one of them a young man with strawberry blond hair?"

"Yes, he looked to be about fifteen."

"That was my brother, the older man is our foreman and the other man one of our hands." She turned to the large man, "This is my uncle, Clem Cameron and his son Lars. I am Carmen Cameron, they call me Cam. We have the Double C ranch just over the ridge to the west." The men nodded to Luta.

"I am Lu…Lou Schroeder. On my way home, which is a half days ride north of Denver." He had wanted to say Luta but it just came out Lou and he didn't correct it. The riders made their way down the bank to the deer trail. Patty had stopped and was standing as if she were waiting for them to finish their talk and follow her.

After a mile or more they topped a ridge and Luta looked down upon a grassy meadow, lined with aspen trees. As they rode he noticed several clusters of cattle and horses grazing on the rich grass. At the head of the valley up against a steep sandstone wall was the main house. A log home with a long porch facing the east. Below it were several pole corrals, a loafing shed and barn. Off to one side was a log bunkhouse and an outbuilding.

A windmill, a four legged wooden structure twenty-five to thirty feet in height pumped water into a large wood trough. Part of the trough was in two of the corrals and one side faced the hitch rail. The wheel of the windmill was a circle of wood slats radiating from a shaft and set at angles. It had a vane or tail to turn it into the wind. Set over a well it produced water whenever the wind blew.

A slight breeze was blowing from the west and the smell of wood smoke was strong in the air. As they got nearer, Luta could see the smoke coming out from under the roof of a smoke house at the top of a gentle hill behind the bunkhouse.

"Water your horses and tie up at the hitch rail." She opened the gate to one of the corrals and Patty went in and straight to the water trough. Lars took her and his dad's horse to the barn. Lucky and Duke drank heartily from the trough. Luta saw a tin cup hanging on a nail on a leg of the windmill and used it to get a drink from the wooden spout.

"Patty is getting old and rather long in the tooth. She was my first saddle horse, has the run of the place and must have gotten spooked when the rustlers cut out the cows last night."

Lars came back leading the three horses. He stripped off their bridles and turned them in with Patty. They also went straight to the trough. He got a pitchfork of hay from the loafing shed and pitched it over the pole fence to the horses.

"Patty is a nice looking paint." Luta hung the tin cup back up on the leg of the windmill.

"Thanks, that is a nice black gelding, what is his blood line?" She was looking Lucky over with the trained eye of a horse lover.

"He is three quarter Tennessee Walker, and one quarter mustang. He tends to favor his grand dad." Luta walked to the hitch rail and dropped Lucky's rein over the pole and tied Duke's lead rope with a half-hitch.

"You have any young studs with his conformation for sale?"

"I don't but my uncle and his partner have a few." Luta loosened the girth on Lucky's saddle and did the same to Duke's pack saddle.

"I would be interested in a three or four year old that has some foals on the ground." She was still looking at Lucky while they talked.

"I think they have a couple like that."

"You said a half day's ride north of Denver?"

"Yes, I am guessing it would be about straight west of here a couple long days ride." Luta took his canteen out of Duke's pack. "That is good water, think I will fill my canteen if it's okay."

"Sure. Yes, it is good water. My dad said they tapped into an underground spring." Luta dumped out the water he had and went to the spout to refill his canteen.

"I would like to see what they have for sale but I wouldn't want to leave here until the guys get back with the stolen cows. That could be later today or not for a couple days."

"I am not in any hurry, guess I can wait."

"Lars, please show him an empty bunk."

There were several empty bunks to pick from, Luta took one near a window. The bunk house was large and clean with a long table and kitchen at one end. There was a card table with an old ear marked deck of cards on it.

CHAPTER ELEVEN

Wade and Kemp topped the ridge and looked down on the ranch. At the head of the valley up against a steep sandstone wall was the main house. A log home with a long porch facing the east. Below it were several pole corrals, a loafing shed and barn. Off to one side was a log bunkhouse and an outbuilding.

Following an old deer trail they made their way into the ranch yard. As they approached one of the corrals they both noticed a horse.

"That sure looks like Duke. Can't see his brand but I would bet my last dollar that's Duke." Wade saw a young lady and an older man come out of the main house and walk toward them.

"Howdy, we are looking for a young man riding a big black gelding."

"We are also. We lost his tracks up near the Wyoming border." The young lady had her eyes on Wade's horse more than on him.

"Lost his tracks? Why were you following him?" Kemp folded his hands on the saddle horn and leaned forward.

"He killed one of our hands and run off in the night." The older man stroked his goatee as if it were a nervous habit.

"Killed one of your hands? How did that happen?"

"They were drinking whiskey and playing poker and he accused the man of cheating. We didn't see it but were told our man went for his gun and quick as a cat he threw his bowie knife into the man's throat. Grabbed his black and rode off."

"Luta drinking whiskey?" Kemp looked at Wade as he spoke.

"Boy said his name was Lou and yes he sure enough was drinking whiskey as the bottle and his black was about all he took when he rode out. His bedroll is still in the bunkhouse and his pack horse is over there in the corral." She nodded toward Duke in the Carrol.

"I'm his Pa, Kemp Schroeder and this is his uncle Wade Wilbur. Luta has been gone for about a month, he was going off to see where his father was killed and where his mother was captured by the Cheyenne. We began to worry about him and the women folk sent us to see if we could find him."

"Why don't you step down, give your mounts a drink and tie them at the hitch rail? Come up on the porch and we can talk." She nodded toward the windmill.

Later on the porch with some fresh coffee to sip on, she explained how they had come upon Lou. How she had been interested in a stud horse and how he had agreed to stay on and then guide them to this ranch a half days ride north of Denver.

Kemp explained how Luta's mother had been captured by the Cheyenne and his father killed at Sand Creek. How Luta had been raised in the valley had never drank before or showed any sign of aggression.

"We don't know where he has been for the past month or what he has been doing but this is so hard for me to understand."

"Well, for what it's worth. One of the hands did say that Lou said he didn't drink. But later they said he took a glass and appeared to really like it. He took the bottle with him. He rode out without a bridle or saddle. But later in the night came back and got his bridle and saddle without waking anyone. We followed his tracks in the morning but at the river we couldn't find any sign where he came out. We rode both banks for a mile in each direction and couldn't find any sign."

"If you don't mind we will take his things and see if we can cut his trail. He may loop around and head back to the valley. If we find him, you have my word that we will bring him back to answer any charges. If you can, I would be very interested to learn if the man was cheating and if Luta acted in self-defense or if he was the aggressor."

"We will look into it in greater detail. We were most interested in getting on the trail this morning but from what I gathered, the man did cheat and he did go for his gun." Cam took the makings from her shirt pocket. "Anyone care for a smoke?"

"No thinks, never got into the habit."

Photo by Ken Wilbur

Cam rolled herself a cigarette. "I grew up rolling them for my dad. I like to roll them so much I started smoking them." With a wood match she put a flame to her fashioned smoke and took a drag.

"It does not surprise me that he called the man out for cheating, or that he defended himself. But it does surprise me that he ran off. He was not raised that way." Kemp took his hat off the back of his chair, turned and walked down the steps to the ground.

"I do have a couple nice young stallions. One of them has several nice foals on the ground. Both of them have the conformation and disposition of their granddad which is much like the gelding I am riding or the one Luta was riding. "Putting on his hat he followed Kemp to the corral where Duke was pawing the ground.

"Well, I am interested. Keep me informed." She walked to the corral and spoke to one of the hands. "Get his bedroll and pack from the tack room." The cowboy hurried to get Luta's things and bring them to the corral. Duke seemed to know the men and horses and was anxious to get out of his little pole prison.

Once packed up and mounted it was not difficult to see the tracks of the big gelding going north at a full gallop. After a quarter mile or so, they found where he stopped, made a circle to the east at a walk going back toward the building site. They saw in the tall grass where he had went on foot and returned dragging the saddle from time to time. His boot prints going from the head of Lucky back to his side. Once mounted, Luta continued north at a fast walk.

They had no trouble finding where he and several other riders entered the Platte River. They also found the tracks going both north and south on the far bank. "I think it would be best if we go away from the river a quarter mile and see if we can pick up his sign." Wade had turned his horse away from the river.

"I agree. Think we should stay together or split up?" Kemp and Wade were both looking at the lay of the land, trying to picture how it could look in the dark of the night.

"Let's stay together. If we get out of sight of each other and one of us does find something we would have to fire a shot and I really don't want to do that. I don't know why, but a hunch tells me he would go to the northwest."

After a half hour they came to a road. They followed it to the north. An hour later they saw a small town the sign on the outskirts said, Carpenter, WY. 68. It had just one street. It looked like business places on the north and homes on the south. In the middle on the north side of the street was a saloon, the Water Hole. They tied up at the hitch rail and went in.

"Two beers please." Wade reached in his pocket and found a couple nickels. "Looking for a young man who may have been in here earlier. Wearing a red kerchief and black flat hat."

"Ye, he was here. Jumpy as a jackrabbit. Had him one drink and he went over to the General Store. Saw him ride out going north a spell later." The bartender was a big man going bald but with a face full of hair. "He in some kind of trouble?"

"No, he's my son. We were to meet up but we missed him and we think he thinks we are ahead of him." Wade looked at Kemp with a little smile thinking that he was the worse liar he had ever heard. They drank their beer, thanked the barkeep and went next door to the General Store.

"Looking for my boy. Eighteen, wearing a black flat hat and a red kerchief."

"Yes, he was in. Got a few supplies. Seemed to be in a hurry. Didn't even wait for his change. It was only eight cents but eight cents is eight cents." The clerk was a thin man, had his glasses up on his forehead. He was wearing a white apron that looked like it had not been changed for several days. "You want the change?"

"No. If he didn't take it, he meant it for you."

CHAPTER TWELVE

Luta rode north through fertile valleys many with high red rock walls. He was making a circle, heading back north toward Johnson County where he had been a week before. He did not sleep well, he had nightmares. He was always pulling his bowie knife out of the throat of the dying cowboy. Blood gushing out over his hand as he retrieved the weapon. He would wake up in a sweat, breathing hard and sit up with a jerk not sure where he was for a few seconds.

His days were long, he would ride from sun up to sun down. He crossed the Sweetwater River riding into the Granite Mountains. The granite was light-gray to reddish-gray and the rounded knobs and hills rose a few hundred yards above the flat plain. From time to time he would find an oasis of aspens, gurgling water coming out of the rock and disappearing again into the granite.

It was at one of these oasis that he was making camp. He had learned in the past couple weeks that people perceived him very different depending on his name or what they knew about him. He was now experiencing a new way of looking at himself. He felt different and he didn't like this new Luta. He wanted to go back to the valley but he couldn't make himself ride in that direction. He wished it would be like it was, but he felt it could never be like that again. He could just see Squirt with that, "I told you so...." look on her face. She would be as disappointed in him as he was in himself.

It had all happened so fast. He had seen the card palmed and he called the man before he gave it a thought. When he saw him start for his colt, he just reacted. He couldn't figure out how he got the Bowie in his hand so fast. He must have absentmindedly reached for it when he saw the man palm the card. The cheater was starting to draw his revolver when he saw his Bowie in his throat. The blood gushing out and all the hands screaming and yelling. It had all happened so fast and now it seemed like a bad dream. But it wasn't a bad dream, it really happened, he killed a man.

He pulled the cork on his last bottle of whiskey and took a long pull. It burned all the way down but the warm feeling seemed to dull the pain in his brain.

He had heard about the Willow Creek Ranch, where this rancher had several log cabins in an out of the way valley where outlaws could stay. He was being drawn to it. It seemed like the best place for him to go right now. He didn't want to continue to just ride around and he couldn't make himself go back to the valley or back to the ranch where he killed the young cowboy.

He had lost his appetite, he had no desire for food. He did not sleep well and he didn't even like his own company. He could not even write how he felt in his journal. The only thing that seemed to give him any pleasure was whiskey. He needed a place to sort out his feelings. A place where he could interpret his feelings. He knew there could be risks involved but the risks were unknown and right now he felt like throwing caution to the wind.

A sheep rancher, Kenneth MacDonald, found what he wanted in the red wall country of Johnson County. He had learned the sheep business in Australia. He came to California with a crew to shear sheep for the summer. At the end of the shearing season, the crew sailed home without him. He put together a herd of sheep and learned that it was not popular to be a sheep man in the west in the early 1880's. He needed a way to protect himself and his sheep.

He found this canyon between the Red Wall and the Big Horn Mountains. The area was isolated and a narrow funnel shaped opening was the only way into the canyon from the east. The valley inside was fertile and the narrow trail over the red wall was easy to defend. Later he got the land just outside the canyon and started the Willow Creek Ranch. In those days there were a great many who rustled cattle for a living. They were being tracked down and hung by the large ranchers or the Wyoming Cattlemen's Association.

MacDonald came up with the idea to let them have the valley, he would bring his sheep out to the Willow Creek Ranch site and they would have protection and they would also protect him and his sheep.

The valley and Buffalo Creek that ran through it, gave them everything they needed. They built several log cabins. It became known as a robbers roost. Bad guys that rustled from the large cattle barons, robbed trains or banks had a place to rest up if they could out-run the posse and get there.

In the late 1880's and early 1890's the inhabitants of this valley were known as the "Hole in the Wall Gang." *

*Several years later, Butch Cassidy and the Sundance Kid were said to stay in the Hole in the Wall.

Luta sat on his haunches staring into the flickering fire. He had not cooked anything. Hadn't not even made coffee.

Since it wasn't cold, he had no need for a fire. The wavering flame seemed to have him in a daze. It was as if he were in a hypnotic trance. A camp fire could be a beautiful flickering friend who reached out with warmth. It could also be a reminder of shame. A torment of punishment, of extreme anguish and pain for the mind that was hard to bear. Luta was finding it was much easier to forgive others than to forgive himself.

He took another long pull on the whiskey. It burned and took his breath away even the whiskey couldn't take away the anguish he felt. He had to trust his gut feeling. He knew the brain could be fooled and that the heart could be stupid but your gut doesn't know how to lie. His gut told him to find this safe place and sort things out.

His gut did not know that the people back at the ranch had learned that he acted in self-defense. His gut perceived him as a murderer. Just as people often get the wrong impression of him, he also get the wrong impression of ourselves.

CHAPTER THIRTEEN

"It's my fault, it's all my fault!"

"Martha, it is no one's fault." Kemp and Wade had stopped in Bear Lake on their way back to the valley. They had told Squirt, Sarah and Dusty what they had found out.

"If I had been supportive, Lou would have come back. It's my fault. It's my fault that he doesn't feel comfortable coming here with his troubles."

"We don't know, we have not been to the valley. He may be there, we lost his trail and couldn't pick it up again. We just stopped here to let you know what we found out."

"Let me gather my things, I am going with you." She ran to her room and Dusty went to saddle her horse. They got to the valley in time for church.

Jokob, the pastor was at the altar. "You want happiness, be useful. You want happiness, be compassionate. You want happiness live your life so that you make a difference for having lived. Don't go looking for happiness.

Look for ways to be useful. Look for ways to be compassionate. Live your life to make a difference and you will be happy. We pray today for our son, brother, grandson, nephew and friend that he will make his way home. Everyone makes mistakes, that doesn't mean they have to pay for them the rest of their life. Living in such a nice peaceful valley we tend to forget how cruel the world can be. How difficult it can be. We ask our Lord to guide Luta back to his family. We ask this in Jesus name. Amen."

Sarah played the doxology and they all sang. She went right into, "Sweet is the Vale."

"There is not in the wide world a valley so sweet.

As the vale in whose bosom the bright waters meet,

Oh! The last rays of feeling and life must deport,

Ere the bloom of the valley shall fade from my heart."*

*Written by Thomas Moore, 1808.

After the service they all joined together for a meal. Pat and Martha did not feel much like eating. Pat had just learned of her son's fate the night before when Kemp got home. Jokob and his wife Sarah had just learned of it this morning before church. Jokob had to change his whole sermon and Sarah had to put on her brave, everything will be fine, face.

Everyone was concerned and everyone made their best attempt at being positive. They all took solace in the fact that the young cowboy had been cheating and that Luta did act in self-defense.

As Squirt walked out of church she was surprised to see Jesse sitting in the shade of the big aspen. "What are you doing here?"

"Dusty told me about your situation and thought maybe you could use a friend."

"What can this friend do?"

"Well, we are delivering two hundred head of cattle to the Wind River Indian Reservation in Wyoming next week and I thought I could keep an eye open for your friend."

"You think he will be at the reservation?"

"No, but we will be covering some of the ground where Dusty said he was last seen. Just wanted you to know that if I did lay eyes on him I would tell him how much you want him to come home." Jesse slowly got to his feet and walked toward Martha. "Dusty said he was riding a big black gelding, wearing a flat black hat and would have a red kerchief around his neck."

"Who all is going on this drive?"

"My Dad, Mom, myself and several other hands."

"Your Mom is going?"

"Yes, she likes to trade with the Indians and she doesn't trust us to get the things she wants. She will drive the chuck wagon"

Martha whirled and went back into the church leaving Jesse standing there wondering what just happened. In a few minutes she came out skipping and smiling from ear to ear.

"I'm going with you. Well, that is, if it is okay with your parents. I can help your Mom drive and fix the meals. I am going crazy waiting and I am a huge pain to everyone around me." She ran to Jesse and gave him a hug. When she realized what she was doing, she stepped back but her joy could not help but shine through.

"I feel sure it will be fine with them. Mom has always wanted a daughter, she will be in her glory." Jesse was amazed at the change in Martha. Hope can do that for a person.

The moon on Bear Lake gave it a magical look. Martha was anxious to get started. The morning could not come soon enough for her. She was staying with Dusty and Sarah, She would join the cattle drive when it came through in the morning. In her mind and heart she knew this was going to be a wonderful trip.

Photo by Rachel Rosenboom

CHAPTER FOURTEEN

Martha was surprised when she saw the cattle. It looked like they had found and rounded up the oldest cows on their ranch. They moved at a slow pace (ten to twelve miles a day). In the back of her mind she felt they didn't have to worry about a stampede. At the end of a day, these cows were just happy to lay down and chew their cud.

She enjoyed Mrs. Collins. Loretta Collins was very organized and never wasted a motion, she seemed to anticipate every need of the men. Loretta and Martha had to get up before the hands to have coffee and sourdough biscuits ready. The chuck wagon was the headquarters of the drive. They ate around it used it was the social center and a place to recount the experiences of the day.

The normal colorful and profane comments did not take place around this chuck wagon. Once in a great while a hand would have a slip of the tongue and utter a profane word but as soon as it came out an apology followed that drew smiles from all in hearing distance.

The wagon was drawn by a team of mules and carried not only their food but a water barrel, tools and the crew's bed rolls. Another difference from most drives was that all the hands went to the wash basin to scrubbe their hands and faces. They used a common comb to arrange messy hair before they got in line for food.

None of the hands complained about the grub or made jokes about the cooks. They would even help gather fire wood and hitch up the mules. They were careful approaching the campsite to stay downwind so they didn't cause dust to blow into the chuck wagon. There was no scuffling or pushing in the food line. They always scraped their plates clean and put them in the receptacle provided.

It was a two week drive to the Wind River Indian Reservation so Martha and Loretta learned a great deal about each other. Martha also learned that the hands respected Jesse. He was the son of the boss but he pulled his weight and got no special privileges. Even his mother didn't give him a little extra meat or a larger piece of pie.

The small herd of two hundred cows would get strung out in a long line. It was always the same old roan cow leading the herd and the same stragglers bringing up the rear. The Indian Agent that contracted for +the cows made it clear he did not want any young cattle. They were to supply food for the winter. The hides would make fine moccasins, vests and coats. The reservation was located in southeastern Wyoming near the town of Horse Creek. This scenic and mountainous reservation was home to about five hundred Arapahoe.

They were just within the exterior boundary of the reservation when a group of riders approached them. It was the Indian Agent and several young tribal members.

"We will take charge of the herd. One of you can come with us to get a final tally and the receipt to take to the Horse Creek Bank. The bank was robbed two days ago but it is my understanding that it is open and doing business." The agent did not look to be comfortable on his horse. His black suit, white shirt and black string tie seemed out of place. He had a bad mustache that he continued to comb with his fingers as if he hoped to make it thicker.

The young men with him were all of medium build, with dark hair and eyes. The color of their eyes was from hazel brown to dark brown and the skin tone was from coppery to bronze. Their hair was straight and slightly coarser than that of the agent. Many had eyebrows that were connected above the nose. All of them tended to all have high cheek bones and were generally handsome. In closer examination their eyes were empty. These young men and the other residents have had to adapt to a clash of culture and long tradition. They were not happy. In fact they were angry.

"We started with two hundred and five. I wanted to have a few extra. I know we lost one to a broken leg." Mr. Collins reached across his horse and extended his hand to the agent. "Jim Collins."

"Herman Husker, I am the Agent for the Wind River Indian reservation and we have a corral about a mile east of here. If your people want, they can go north about a half mile and cut the road into Horse Creek. They will find a nice clean hotel."

"My wife was hoping to do some trading with the Arapahoe."

"There is a trading post in Horse Creek run by the Indians. Just a few doors east of the hotel. They have some very nice things." He made a sweeping motion with his arm to the young men and they spread out to move the cattle.

He was correct, the hotel was nice and clean. Both Mrs. Collins and Martha enjoyed a bath in a tub of sudsy hot water. Their first in over two weeks. It had been a good drive but they were glad that it was over.

Martha coming into the lobby saw Jesse in a big black over-stuffed chair reading the newspaper. When he saw her he quickly folded the paper and put it in the chair behind him. He got to his feet and quickly came to her.

"Have a nice bath? I did and it sure did feel good to get the trail dust off." He was dressed in clean clothes, even had a shine on his boots.

"Yes, I did enjoy the bath. That is the first drive I have been on, it was fun and interesting but I am glad that it is over." She looked at the chair where he had been reading the paper.

"What's in the paper? Anything interesting?"

"Mostly local news and ads for stuff at the General Store. It is a democratic paper so it has nothing good to say about President Arthur. It does have a cartoon about the assassination of James Garfield." Jesse took her hand and made an attempt to lead her toward the door.

"Jesse. What don't you want me to see?" She turned and walked to the chair. Taking the paper, the front page headline caught her attention. "Horse Creek Bank Robbed." She was reading the article when the description of the third bank robber made her drop the paper, "It's Lou! Lou robbed the bank!"

Jesse reached out to her, taking her by her elbows. "Martha, you don't know that for sure. It could be just a coincidence that the robber resembles Luta."

"It is him, that big black horse the black hat and red kerchief......" Her knees buckled and Jesse had to hold her up. He helped her to a chair where she slumped down as if overcome with the information.

"You knew it was Lou, that's why you didn't want me to see it!" She sat with her head in her hands, wanting to cry but tears would not come.

Jesse searched for some comforting answers, but none came to mind. He knelt in front of her, holding her hands. After a few seconds that seemed like hours to Jesse, she sat up.

"I want to take a walk. I need to clear my head. I am sorry that I acted so hysterical." She got to her feet and taking Jesse's arm walked to the door.

They walked, neither of them saying anything. The sun setting behind the tall pine trees gave them comfort. It seemed to be saying there was a higher power watching over them.

Photo by Dale Huggins

CHAPTER FIFTEEN

"The leader was wearing a dark double-breasted suit with a wing collar. He looked more like a drummer then an outlaw. The second man had a very dark complexion, dark hair and eyes, was slight build. This fits what we know about the Logan brothers. The third man was young, wearing a black hat and a red kerchief. He did not carry a revolver but had a Winchester and rode a big black. The posse lost them a half day's ride north of here. We have reason to believe that they are headed for the Hole in the Wall. It is a day's ride from any semblance of civilization. It is in a remote, secluded part of Johnson County." The Sheriff was seated behind a scarred oak desk in his small office.

"You say this, what did you call it, Hole in the Wall is remote?" Martha talked Jesse into going to the Sheriff's office with her. She hardly gave him time to finish his breakfast.

"Yes, it is a remote pass in the Big Horn Mountains." The Sheriff was sipping coffee from a tin cup.

"If you know where this is, will the posse go there?"

"It is impossible to approach without alerting the outlaws and one outlaw can sit up on the rim and hold off a small army. There is no way I can get men to volunteer to go anywhere near it." He leaned back in his chair and put the heel of his boot on the desk. His spur adding another scar.

"So, they just get away?"

"Sooner or later, they will come out. When they do, we will get them." He swung his other leg up, crossed his legs at his ankles and leaned back as if he were ready for a nap.

"Can you draw me a map of your best guess as to where this Hole in the Wall is?" Martha took a step forward to stand before his desk.

"Yes, I guess I could do that." He swung his feet to the floor and reached in a drawer for some paper and a stub of a pencil. His map was not the best but it did show where Horse Creek, Casper and the Hole in the Wall were. "It's about two days ride northwest of here."

"Thank you and thank you for the information. I don't know but I think the third robber could be a friend." She picked up the paper and showed it to Jesse.

"You be very careful if you try to find this hideout. You don't know who will be on guard and he may not be a friend to anyone." The Sheriff stood up and for the first time Martha noticed how short he was. They were about the same height, just a little over five feet.

"You planning to go to this place?" Jesse asked as they were walking back to the hotel.

"I will see if I can talk my father into taking me. I come back to the valley." As they were going up onto the hotel porch, Jim and Loretta Collins were coming out.

"We are going out to the Arapahoe village I want to see if I can do some trading. I didn't see anything in the trading post that interested me. Do you want to come along?" Jesse looked to Martha, she shrugged her shoulders and gave him a little nod of her head.

"Sure, we will go with you. I will help dad get the horses." He turned and walked to the hotel stable with his father. It was not a long ride and topping a ridge they looked down on a cluster of tipis. They saw some women hanging strips of meat on racks to dry. They saw others working with hides from cows. Scraping the flesh off the inside and the hair off the outside. There were children playing and dogs running around the camp. One of the children spotted them up on the ridge and gave a yell they did not understand but caused everyone to look where he was pointing.

Slowly they walked their horses down the slope to the camp. A young brave, he couldn't have been more than twelve came with an old woman to meet them.

"I am Little Beaver. What is it that you want?" His English was rather good and easy to understand.

"I would like to trade some things. I was at the trading post but would rather trade here if anyone wants to trade." Mrs. Collins showed the boy some of the things she had. Silver Conchos, crystal Conchos, colorful buttons, and some belt buckles. The young brave turned to the old woman and spoke to her in Arapahoe.

"Luyu say women in trading post are apples. That she would be happy to trade with you."

"Apples?"

"Yes, the women are red on the outside but white on the inside. Come this way." He turned and followed Luyu to her tipi. Mrs. Collins, Martha, the young brave and Luyu entered the tipi, Jesse and his father stayed with the horses.

Jesse took the opportunity to explain to his father what Martha wanted to do. He told him what they had learned from the Sheriff and about the map.

"She is not going to be happy or satisfied until she lets him know that he can come back to their valley." Jesse took off his hat and hung it on his saddle horn.

"What is it that you want to do?"

"It is a couple days closer from here than from her place, so it makes sense if she is going, to go from here but I don't know if she will go with me alone."

"Your mother is always ready for an adventure. Let me talk to her about this and see what she thinks. You say it is a couple days ride from here?"

"That's what the Sheriff said."

"We could send the crew back with the chuck wagon and take a pack horse and some supplies with us. Going home from there, it would be almost straight south to the Circle C." Jim Collins was a strong family man, his son was the most important thing in the world to him, next to his wife. "You have strong feelings for Martha?"

"Yes. From the first time I saw her in the store."

"How does she feel about you?"

"I think she likes me. This Luta is like a twin brother to her, they grew up together. They are very close and she is worried about him."

CHAPTER SIXTEEN

It was their second day on the trail when they saw a ranch. They had heard the sheep before they saw them. Not a real large flock, a couple hundred head grazed in the fertile valley off the trail. A black and white dog and a single man were with them.

Over the ridge ahead of them they could see a wisp of smoke rising into the windless sky. Riding on, they saw that it came from the chimney of a log cabin. There were several corrals and a couple of small out buildings. A dog that had been laying on the porch came out to greet them. He was also+ black and white and his barking produced a man coming out of the cabin.

Jim Collins did his best to explain why they were there but he did not know how much the man understood. The man seemed to speak English but his accent was strong and difficult for them to understand. They got that his name was MacDonald and that the Hole in the Wall was up a narrow trail in the red wall a quarter mile ahead of them.

Riding nearer the wall, they could see a trail winding upward a quarter mile over loose rocks to the top of the red wall. They could see a slab of white rock at the very top. They saw no sign of life. At the base of the wall they could see tracks leading to the steep trail.

"Hello!" Martha cupped her hands, leaned back and yelled as loud as she could. "Hello!" Nothing. There was no sign of life at the top of the red wall.

"I am going to ride up a ways and then call to them." Martha turned her horse onto the trail leading upward.

"You want me to come with you?" Jesse started to follow her.

"No. I think there is less chance they will shoot if it is just me." Her horse made its way up the steep climb over the loose rocks. She leaned forward over its neck. After several hundred feet of climbing a shot echoed down the canyon wall. She pulled her horse to a halt and looked up but saw no movement.

"Hello!" She yelled as loud as she could. "I came to talk to Lou." She waited but there was nothing from the top of the wall. She started her horse forward again and again a shot echoed down through the canyon.

"I just want to give Lou, Luta a message." She yelled. "I want him to know it is okay to come home." Her horse was getting nervous. It was not comfortable with the starting and stopping on the steep trail. She started forward again and after climbing a hundred feet or so, another shot rang out.

"Please tell Luta to come home!" she yelled at the top of her lungs and it sounded even louder bouncing off the canyon wall. She waited as her nervous horse pawed at the loose rock. She felt sure they had heard her. She was at a place that was wide enough to turn around. The nervous horse was more than happy to change direction. She leaned way back, her toes high in the stirrups to help the horse keep balance going back down the trail.

Once back on the flat land with the others, both Martha and her horse were able to relax. After several long deep breaths to slow down her heart rate, she took a sip of water from her canteen and felt normal again.

"I think you accomplished what you came for. I can now understand what the Sheriff said. One man could hold off a small army trying to go up that steep climb." Jesse rode up next to her. "You okay?"

"Yes. I wish I would have gotten some sign that they heard me." She turned in the saddle to look up the red wall. At the very top next to the slab of white rock she thought she caught sight of movement but she couldn't be sure.

"I think they heard you. I think that flock of sheep heard you." Mr. Collins said with a smile. "Should we head south and find a good place to camp for the night?" Without waiting for anyone to reply he turned his horse back the way they had come.

Martha felt better. She could go back feeling that she had done all that she could do. She had the paper to share with Pat and Kemp, and she could tell them that she had seen this fortified hideout. That she did her best. She was so pleased that Jesse and his parents had gone out of their way for her. She would never be able to thank them. She was disappointed in learning about the bank robbery but that was so much better than staying at home and not knowing anything.

All at once her world looked better. Like Luta, she had not been out of the valley that much. She had not spent any amount of time away from her family in the valley. She had seen and experienced so many new and different things the past three weeks. She had worked harder than at any time in her life and it felt good. She had learned on the face of that red wall that courage was not the absence of fear but overcoming fear to do what had to be done. Now, she better understood that energetic feeling that gives people the power and strength to either escape or attack. All your senses seem to be dramatically heightened and you get this sudden boost of energy. She had never felt that before. She had to admit that she liked the feeling.

Photo by Rachel Rosenboom

Wildlife was abundant bears, mountain lions, moose, deer, elk and it was also prime habitat for rattlers so they had to keep a sharp eye around the rock formations. Soaring over all of them was the Bald Eagle. They were miles from a road but this would shorten their trip home by at least a day. The sunrises and sunsets were often spectacular as the colors radiated across the horizon. Martha found herself thinking more about Jesse and less about Lou as the days passed.

CHAPTER SEVENTEEN

Chet was banned from the cabin. Carmen was in labor, Judith, and her mother were taking charge. It would be Judith's first grandchild and Sarah's first great grandchild. Sarah had been a midwife many times but this time it was special. Doctors were often, as in this case, a half days ride away. The women viewed birth as a part of nature but they didn't face it with joy and ecstasy.

He knew Carmen was in good hands, his mother and his grandmother routinely provided medical care for their families.

Chet paced the porch wondering what was going on in the cabin. Weird and negative thoughts flying through his mind. Death during childbearing was always a possibility for both the baby and the mother.

After what seemed like hours he heard a baby cry. It was a loud strong cry which he knew was a good sign but it still sent chills through his body. It was even worse when the crying stopped. He wanted to race to Carmen's bedside, he strained but could hear nothing but the beating of his heart and his heavy breathing. His mouth was dry and he felt a little light headed.

The door opened and his mom stuck her head out. "Both mother and baby boy are doing fine. Give us a few minutes and you can come in." Without waiting for him to say anything she disappeared back into the cabin.

"Oh, thank you Lord." He looked up to see the splendor of a glittering star filled sky. The stars glowed so brightly they seemed to illuminate the rugged Colorado landscape. The valley never looked so good to him, he had a son. Was he ready to be a father? Moments ago he was worried about Carmen and a healthy baby. Now he felt shocked, a little panicked, scared of being a father. Would his mother and grandmother leave him to care for Carmen and the baby? Would he have to change a diaper?

"Chet, you can come in now." His mother was holding the door open for him to enter. "Carmen is feeling tired and needs to sleep so don't plan to stay too long."

Chet couldn't take his eyes off the little bundle lying beside Carmen. The baby had a stock of black hair that seemed to go in every direction, chubby cheeks and no neck. He was red and his face a little puffy. Chet bent over the bed and kissed Carmen on the forehead and then on the lips.

"Want to hold your son?" Carmen asked with a proud smile. "Ah. Yes." He slide his right hand under the baby's head and shoulders and his left hand around and under his butt. He lifted him up and turned so the light from the lamp shown on his face. "Carlos, what do you think of the place?"

"Is Carlos what you want to call him?"

"Yes, if it is okay with you."

"Dad would be so proud and honored." Carmen was tired but the thought of her father made her face lit up with joy. Chet looked down at his son and thought of that day several years ago.

On a knoll, under a large cottonwood tree, they dug the grave. Chet and Shad made it deep, cutting through roots and removing rocks so as to insure its safety. Joss used a hot branding iron to burn his name and the date on a wooden cross. When they were finished, Carmen placed his saddle in the grave, they wrapped Carlos in a wagon sheet with his head on the saddle. They covered the body. The grave overlooked a meadow, gorgeous with a mass of wild flowers. They were still in Texas, which would please Carlos.

Carmen was being as brave as could be expected until Shad began to sob. This caused her to break down, weeping in grief for her father. These were tough drovers, but there wasn't a dry eye among them. Joss read from his Bible and asked the Lord to take in his cousin and friend.

The drovers slowly and silently went back to the herd. It was over an hour before Chet noticed Carmen, leading her father's horse, riding up from the south. She had wanted to remain alone at the grave.

Carmen looked at the melancholy look on Chet's face and she too thought back to the cattle drive and her father's grave in north Texas. They couldn't bring him back but they could keep his memory alive in their newborn son. Little Carlos began to squirm and gnaw at his hand. He started to cry but continued to gnaw at his hand.

"Your son is telling you that he is hungry. Give him to his mother and then they can both rest." Sarah moved a chair beside the bed. "You can sit too, I heard you pacing on the porch. Your mother and I will be in the next room if you need us." Little Carlos nursed and then the three of them took a much needed nap.

CHAPTER EIGHTEEN

Luta rode into the hidden valley from the north, came down the west wall and rode up toward the east end. He stripped the saddle off Lucky and turned him loose. There were several bunches of cows with calves grazing in the valley. Picking up his tack he went to the door leading into Sweeny's barn. Opening the door, he surprised Sweeny who was cleaning out a stall.

"Hey! You trying to get yourself shot?" Sweeny had dropped his fork and was reaching for his colt.

"Trying to keep from getting shot. I thought it best to come in the back way, too much travel on that road east of here." Luta dropped his stuff and took Sweeny's out stretched hand.

"Bring your stuff in here, got an extra saddle tree you can use." He turned and went into the tack room. "The women are all over at Chet's. He and Carmen had a little boy last night. Wade was going to stop in to see his grandson and then check the stock at the north end of the valley. Don't rightly know what your Pa is doing this morning. Your mom and sister went with Penny in the buckboard."

Luta put his saddle on the tree, hung the bridle over the horn and put the saddle blanket on top. His bedroll was still on the back of his saddle and Winchester in the scabbard. He took off his hat, knocked the dust off it on his leg, brushed it with his hand and replaced it on his head.

"Guess I got some explaining to do." He went on to tell Sweeny about the card game.

"Your Pa and Wade were at that ranch, they told them that the range hand was cheating and that you acted in self-defense. They picked up Duke and your things but lost your trail around the border to Wyoming."

"So everyone knows about the killing?" Luta seemed relieved that he didn't have to tell the story over and over.

"Yes, and the bank robbery." Sweeny could see the surprised look on Luta's face.

"How did Squirt get up to the Hole in the Wall and who was that with her?" Luta took a seat on a feed sack.

Sweeny explained how Martha had gone on the cattle drive to the Wind River reservation, saw the newspaper in Horse Creek and talked them into going with her up to give you the message to come home.

"How did she get on with the Circle C drive?"

"She met the son of Old Man Collins at Bear Lake and found out they were taking cattle up there. She talked them into letting her go along, hoping to talk to someone that had seen you. The Horse Creek newspaper had the story of the bank robbery and your description in it. The Sheriff told her he figured the gang went to the Hole in the Wall. She talked Collins, his wife and son into going with her."

"So they know it all. They know what a mess I made of everything."

"Well they don't know what you are going to do now. I am sure they will be glad to see you and learn what your plans are."

"I don't know. I thought I was guilty of murder, I never dreamed that the people at the ranch would tell the truth. I didn't have a plan when I came here and I really don't know what to do now. I will have to talk with Pa and my Mom, see what they think I should do." He sat on the feed sack, head in his hands, thinking how life would be so much simpler if he had not gone on the trip. Home, there is magic in that little word, he already felt the comfort and virtue of the valley. He realized now that he had to leave the valley to see how great it was.

"Take your time. I got some things to do. If I see Kemp I will tell him you are here. I don't know how long the women will be gone." Sweeny went back into the barn leaving Luta to sort out his feelings.

It was a long night, with more talk than Luta wanted to hear or take part in. When it was finally time for him to go to his room he was thankful for the feeling of family. It gave him strength and courage. He still had to face Squirt, she was in Bear Lake and he didn't know when she would be back. Chet had told the women that he would ride and tell Sarah, Dusty and Squirt the news and register the birth certificate the first thing in the morning. Judith was staying to help Carmen for a few days.

The next morning at the breakfast table. "I know it is the right thing to do, but I am worried they will be prejudice against you." Pat refilled Kemp and Luta's coffee cups.

"I agree that it will be difficult to get an impartial jury if they find out Luta is half Cheyenne. I think it could be best to wave the jury trial and put our faith in the judge." Kemp reached for another piece of toast.

"What do you know about the District Court Judge?" Pat put the coffee pot on the back of the stove and returned to the table.

"Nothing, but I am sure that we can find out who it is and a little about him." Kemp was putting some of Pat's blackberry jam on his toast.

"Well, we really don't have much of a choice. As I see it, I either have to take my chances with the court or continue to run and be an outlaw. I have seen enough of that life to know I prefer living in the valley." Luta sipped his hot coffee.

"You could stay here and do nothing. The people at the ranch are not going to put the law on you and no one knows you were in the Horse Creek bank robbery." Pat was thinking like a mother.

"I know. You know. The whole valley knows and until the court says it was self-defense I will always feel like it was murder." Luta had been living with this feeling every step he took and it was not a feeling he wanted for the rest of his life.

"Luta you have to be prepared for the worst. The court could find you guilty and you would be sent to Yuma Territorial Prison or they could find you not guilty and send you to a reservation in Oklahoma just for being half Cheyenne."

"Your mother is right Luta, some people are very prejudiced."

"I know, I found that out on my trip. I was treated different when they knew my name was Luta than if they thought it was Lou. I was a totally different person in their eyes with just a name change. Being half Cheyenne made me bad, dangerous. I need to find out if what I did was murder or self-defense."

CHAPTER NINETEEN

Fort Collins had been a buzz for days. It was the first murder trial the town had ever had and the interest was high. The local newspaper, The Fort Collins Messenger, had an account of the card game with a cartoon of a man pulling a knife out of the throat of another man who had his gun drawn. The Sheriff had talked to the circuit judge and they were going to hold the trial in the new opera house. It had stone pillars and an arch over the main entrance. It was the largest building in Fort Collins and it was where they would examine the evidence and decide the fate of Luta.

Three weeks earlier Luta had a face to face with Squirt for the first time in months. The glory of a friendship is not an outstretched hand, a hug or a kindly smile. It is what comes when you discover that someone believes in you and is willing to trust you with their friendship. A true friend is a rare treasure. Luta knew when Squirt came to the Hole in the Wall and gave him the message to come home that she indeed was a true friend. She had come to rescue him. He wished he had a way to show her that his feelings were also unconditional. He did his best with his first words to her.

"You were right. I should have listened to you. I am so sorry that I put you through this. Can you ever forgive me for being so stupid and pigheaded?"

"Nothing to forgive you for. I am not your friend when you do what I say or when what you do turns out good. I am your friend in good times or in crisis."

They talked for hours about what they had done and about what the future may hold for them. Luta explained all the circumstances that his mother had pointed out.

"Sounds like more bad things can happen than good. You sure this is essential for you to move on with your life?" Deep in her heart, she knew the answer to that before she asked him the question. Their friendship started the moment they began socializing, it was almost as if they were twins. They had a feeling of comfort and emotional safety with each other. They did not have to weigh their thoughts or measure their words, in fact it was almost like they knew what the other was thinking.

They didn't speak of Jesse much. Luta asked if he was respectful and Squirt told him that he was very respectful. Luta nodded his head as if to say that's good enough for me.

Luta was keeping to the valley and letting his Pa and Wade handle the legal arrangements. He was keeping busy working the cattle and horses. Squirt would help him when she was in the valley but she would often go to Bear Lake to help Dusty and Sarah with their store.

Kemp had taken a young stallion to the Double C ranch and told them that he had arranged for Luta to give himself up to the Sheriff in Fort Collins. He told them that the young stud was not a bribe to get them to testify in court but for payment for what they had already done. He expressed how grateful he and his wife were to hear that their son acted in self-defense. They both knew how easy it would be for a ranch to take the side of their hand over a stranger.

"Well, thank you for this fine looking young stud. I feel we should pay you something for bringing him all this way." Cam extended her hand to Kemp.

"I had to see the Sheriff in Fort Collins anyway. Hope this guy gives you some fine foals. Like I said before, we are very grateful for your honest opinion of what happened."

It was after he had talked with the Sheriff and made arrangements to bring Luta in that he heard some bad news. He had not eaten anything but jerky and water for two days and wanted a meal before heading back to the valley. He was enjoying a steak in the hotel dining room when he overheard some men talking at the next table.

"Who knows how many those Cheyenne Dog Soldiers killed?" The three men were all dressed in suits, very dark gray almost black with matching vests and white shirts with wing collars. They looked like they had all ordered from the same catalogue.

"I thought all the Indians were confined to reservations. What's this guy doing running around?" They could be traveling drummers selling anything from snake oil to church organs.

"I heard he was raised by white folks west of here. Guess he went on the war path." His laugh had an annoying childish whine to it.

"Well I am guessing it won't take a jury long to find the cockroach guilty."

"Sure would like to stay around and watch him swing but I got to get down the road and make some money." He had a leather sample bag at his feet.

"You make any money peddling whiskey?"

"Yeah, the Bear Grass Bourbon is my best seller. Some of the better hotels will buy the California Club. Most of the bars just want the cheap rotgut." He pushed his plate away from him and reached in his coat for a cigar.

"Here smoke a real cigar," the man to his left handed him one from his coat.

"Crack Shot?"

"Yes, made up in Canada. One of my best sellers."

"I should pick up a cigar line and sell it along with my whiskey. At the very least I could smoke my samples." He put a match to the cigar and took a deep drag.

"Yes, I am making my first trip west of the Mississippi River. It is inconceivable how much empty space is out here and lack of formal government. Will they really hang this man if he is found guilty?"

"Lucky he hasn't been hung already. Most think the only good injun is a dead injun." He was doing a very poor job of blowing smoke rings.

"I thought all that existed only in dime novels and in campfire tales."

"These decent folks have overcome many hardships. They've seen or experienced Indian massacres. That is not an easy thing to forget. The best he can hope for is to be sent to an Indian Reservation. He wouldn't last a week in Yuma."

"You don't think he has a chance to be found not guilty. I heard something about self-defense."

"He's an Indian, they are not going to just turn him loose. If he were Arapaho they might send him up to Wind River but being he is Cheyenne he will be sent to Oklahoma."

Kemp had a sick feeling, he could not finish his steak. This was what he and Pat had feared but they wanted to believe that Luta was different. He didn't look Indian, he didn't talk or act Indian. They had hoped that the court and the people would take this into consideration. He now realized Luta was going into court and the only way he would come out was guilty of murder or guilty of being an Indian.

CHAPTER TWENTY

Samuel Hastings sat behind a raised desk that served as his bench. Behind the judge were the flags of the United States and the state of Colorado. He was wearing a plain black robe and held a small gavel in his right hand. The bailiff stood behind Luta seated in a chair to the right of the judge.

The theater seats of the opera house were full and a number of folks stood in the back against the wall. There was a podium to the judges left where witnesses could stand to address the court. The judge banged his gavel and asked for order.

"Order! Order in my court." The signal for attention fell over the crowd of concerned citizens wanting to see their brand of justice.

"The defendant will rise and state his name for the court." Again Judge Hastings banged his gavel to silence the crowd.

"Luta Schroeder."

"What charges are against this man?"

The Sheriff went to the podium, "The defendant is charged with the murder of Johnny Hunt in a dispute over a card game."

"What have you to say for yourself?" At this point the crowd was a little restless and the judge banged his gavel. "Go to the podium and the bailiff will swear you in."

Luta went to the podium, put his left hand on the bible and raised his right hand to be sworn in. He then went on to tell the court about the card game, the fact that he called Hunt out for cheating and how he threw his knife when Hunt went for his gun. He explained that he was confused and ran but that he had turned himself in to the Sheriff. He returned to his chair and took his seat.

"Being that Mr. Hunt cannot speak for himself, is there anyone here that saw this and can either confirm or dispute this testimony?"

"Yes your honor." One of the cowhands that was in the card game was in the front row and stood up.

"Go to the podium, state your name and be sworn in."

The young cowhand went to the podium where the bailiff held the bible. "Tom Berner."

"Do you swear to tell the truth, the whole truth and nothing but the truth, so help you God?"

"I do." He took his hand off the bible and turned toward the judge. "It happened just as he said it did. We all knew that Johnny would cheat once in a while when he was losing and he would put up a good front when he was called. This time he got more than he bargained for." The Double C hand returned to his chair.

"Do we have any additional testimony that will shed light on this case?" The judge surveyed the crowd while waiting for someone to speak up. "If we have no other evidence I will take a short recess and give you my verdict." He stood up and when he did the whole crowd got to their feet. He turned and walked out of a door behind the flags.

The room became a confused sound of many excited people talking all at once and it got louder and louder but it all stopped when the judge entered the room. The bailiff yelled, "All stand for the honorable Samuel Hastings." The noise of shuffling feet filled the room as the judge took his seat behind the bench.

"You may be seated. Will the defendant remain standing?" Again the noise of people moving to get comfortable filled the room and then there was silence as they awaited the judge's decision.

"After careful consideration of the evidence and circumstances of this case I find the defendant, Luta Schroeder not guilty of murder." The courtroom was a tinderbox and the uproar was deafening but it was drown out by a louder sound, the banging of the judge's gavel on the oak desk. "Order! I want order in this court room." It was silent as a tomb.

"I am concerned for the safety of Mr. Schroeder because of my verdict. Therefore the acquitted will remain in the custody of the Sheriff until he can be turned over to the Indian agent. I am also concerned about people stirring up violence so I am ordering the Sheriff to place anyone inciting violence in jail to face charges when I return in two weeks. Sheriff please take charge of the acquitted." He banged his gavel and rose to his feet.

Later that afternoon, Pat and Kemp were able to speak to Judge Hastings in the hotel lobby. "I am aware of your son's circumstances, but the law is very clear. All Indians are to be confined to reservations."

"Luta will be an outcast, he will be rejected. Is there anything that we can do? Any law that we can take advantage of?" Pat was still in a state of shock.

"Indian agents have many challenges, one being law and order on the reservations. They are in great need of Indian police and judges to help preserve this. They are also in great need of teachers. The army had a need for Indian scouts but this has lessened as most Indians are now on reservations. There is a great deal of fraud and corruption in Indian affairs. I would suggest that you speak with the Indian agent see if he has any suggestions."

Pat and Kemp thanked the judge and made their way to the jail, the town was still humming with excitement. People everywhere were talking about the judge's verdict. Most did not agree with it and those that did were not speaking up. The town wanted to see an Indian hung. They were disappointed when they saw Luta in the court room. He did not look anything like what they expected. They had heard about this half-breed Cheyenne that had killed a white cowhand in a card game, he did not look anything like they imagined. Being a half-breed was all they needed to hear to know that he should swing from the first cottonwood big enough to hold him. Now the judge had spoiled their fun with his verdict.

There were two deputies standing outside the locked door with scatter guns and another just inside. The Sheriff was seated at his desk when they entered.

"We would like to speak with our son if we could and we would also like to thank you for this protection." Kemp and Pat stood arm in arm before the Sheriff.

"You got any weapons on ya?" He got to his feet and nodded to another deputy who was by the cell block door.

"No we are unarmed." Kemp held open his coat so they could see his waist.

The deputy swung open the door for them to enter. Luta was in the first cell, the other two were empty. When he saw them he got to his feet and came to the barred door.

"Thought you would be on your way back to the valley. Squirt was here a few minutes ago with Wade." He gave his mom the best hug he could through the bars.

"We talked with the judge. He suggested we talk with the Indian agent. How are you doing?" His mother held his hands and gave them a squeeze.

"Like I told Squirt. I am the best I have been since this happened. I was found not guilty and I feel very relieved. I feel set free even if I am behind bars." He had a smile on his face and a gleam in his eyes.

"The judge said that you could be a police office, a teacher, or even a judge as they needed all of those. We will talk….." Luta interrupted her. "Let's not worry about that right now, the important thing is I was judged and found not guilty. Go home give Caroline the good news and tell her that her big brother loves her."

He gave his mother the best hug he could between the bars, shook hands with his Pa and watched as they walked out of the jail. He was going into this new adventure with a positive attitude.

CHAPTER TWENTY-ONE

The thing about an adventure is, they rarely involve easy journeys or care-free times. It is often a struggle to overcome adversity that defines us and puts our lives on a path much different than it otherwise might take. That's how it was for Luta.

The Tongue River forms the eastern boundary of the Northern Cheyenne Indian Reservation and Pumpkin Creek as the west boundary. The river basin is shaped like a large shallow bowl, with the west boundary rock formations lying up against the Big Horn Mountains. The basin is often covered with pines but changes its appearance to grassy rolling hills as it approaches the Tongue River. The Tongue River forms cliffs, buttes and bluffs of sandstone with reddish bands running through them. This is an environment in which wild game thrives. There are large numbers of whitetail deer, mule deer, antelope, herds of elk, bear and mountain lions.

Before the railroads and the buffalo hunters this basin was formerly the home of vast migratory herds of American Bison. They would migrate north during the summer months to feed on the grasslands. The Cheyenne followed these herds, coming north in the spring and going south following the herds for the winter. The reason being, the cold waves would freeze the lakes and rivers and temperatures were often well below zero and accompanied by strong winds with blowing snow.

Because they migrated with the buffalo they lived in lodges made of poles covered with buffalo skin. These tipis could be disassembled and packed away quickly when the tribe needed to relocate. They were warm in the winter and cool in the heat of the summer. Designed with smoke flaps at the top so that they could have a small open fire in the center to cook and warm the lodge. The smoke would exit the top of the tipi and the smoke flaps would prevent a downdraft by the wind. The base of the tipi was about twelve or thirteen feet in diameter, it was roomy and comfortable.

This was a vast space of worthless wasteland from November to April each year. But now the Cheyenne were forced to live here the year around.

This is where Luta found himself. His problem was, he did not have a tipi and he did not have any friends. In fact he was an outcast. He was not even an apple. He didn't even look Indian on the outside. He looked white on the outside and inside. He could not even speak their language. He knew some words and could understand a few more than he could speak but not enough to have an exchange of thoughts.

He had thoughts of helping these people. He felt that he could negotiate for them. Show them how to build log shelters. He had dreams of helping them improve their lives. Raise cattle and horses. He told his mother that it was their fault if they were ungrateful but it was his if he did not try. The little knowledge he had of their language was enough for him to know that he was not welcome. The Indian agent had told him that they would grudgingly accept him. That they were a proud people and for him not to be too aggressive.

Luta liked a challenge but his first adventure had taught him that things were not always as they seemed to be. Luta knew that many white people saw the Indians as uncivilized savages and he was learning that the Indians saw the white man as a conqueror, a liar and not to be trusted. The Indians were promised to be given a yearly payment that would include money, food, livestock, household goods and farming tools. Once the Indians were on the reservation they were forgotten about and the treaties were not adhered to. The white man made no effort to understand their culture.

The horse was the Cheyenne warrior's most important possession. They were skilled horsemen, developing abilities that helped them when raiding, fighting and hunting. Horses enabled tribes to abandon farming and full-time settlements in favor of becoming nomads, roaming the plains in pursuit of the buffalo herds. The Cheyenne quickly adopted to this horse-culture. They became proficient hunters and warriors on horseback.

Now they were being forced onto reservations and back to a culture they did not take pride in. The goal of Indian affairs was to turn the American Indian into a stockman or farmer. To these Indians, Luta was a prime example of this. He was everything they did not want to be. He knew he would fail miserably if he stayed. They would have to teach him before he could hope to teach them. He would have to learn how to make a tipi, how to make a bow and arrows. He would have to learn to be a Cheyenne before he could teach them how to be a cattleman or have a horse ranch.

He stood out here on the reservation like a sore thumb and the agent told him that if he was caught off the reservation he could end up in Yuma. There was only one place he knew where he could fit in. He mounted Lucky and rode east.

The next morning he came to a small community that had a combination general store, post office and tavern all in one. The night before by his camp fire, he had written Squirt and his parents each a letter hoping they would understand his situation. He posted the two letters and purchased a Winchester model 1873 - 44-40 caliber for eleven dollars and a hundred shells for a dollar forty. He found a nice Arkansaw Bowie knife with a buck-horn handle and a seven inch blade for eighty-five cents. A sheep lined coat with a full six inch sheep lined collar for three dollars and fifty cents. He handed the man a twenty dollar gold piece and got four dollars and a nickel in change. He gave him the nickel and took five licorice candy sticks from the jar by the register.

He and Lucky were only on the road a couple hours when he heard shots coming from the south. He topped a ridge and saw a brightly painted Conestoga wagon under fire by what looked to be four or five Indians. He pulled his Winchester, checked the rear sight and levered a shell into the chamber. He had no idea how the new rifle would shoot and not wanting to kill anyone by accident he picked out a rock over the head of the Indians and fired. The ricochet got their attention and Luta noted that the new Winchester shot a little low and to the right.

He levered in another cartridge and this time using a little Kentucky wind age shot at a spot just in front of them kicking dirt up in their faces. This was enough to discourage them and they ran to their horses, hiden in the brush just up the ravine. He waited a few seconds and heard them ride off to the south.

Keeping his Winchester in his hand he rode toward the wagon. He could see one of the mules had been shot and was down, legs thrashing violently, as it was dying from gunshot wounds. He could see no movement. It appeared someone was cooking when attacked. There was a small fire and a large black cast iron skillet was balanced on three rocks over the fire. Luta could smell the meat as he rode up.

The Conestoga wagon was eighteen feet long, ten to twelve feet tall and four feet in width. It was designed to haul freight over the prairie, this one was painted up like a circus wagon. It had a painting of a coiled rattlesnake on the canvas with "DR. Richard" over it and "Snake Oil Promotions" under it.

Luta could see the muzzle of a rifle coming out the opening under the swing seat of the wagon. As he got nearer he could see the dead body of a man on the ground behind the dying mule. He looked to be Mexican but it was difficult to tell as a bullet had hit him on the cheek bone and his face was covered with blood. He now heard a weak voice asking for help coming from the wagon. He dismounted and with caution approached the wagon. Being careful and listening for any warning signs he lifted the corner of the canvas so that he could see in the wagon.

He saw what appeared to be Dr. Richard, he was dressed in a black double breasted suit, white shirt with winged collar and a black string tie. He had a large, waxed handle bar mustache that curved upward and he appeared to have been shot at least twice. Once high on his right arm and once in his lower chest. His tall black stovepipe hat was still on his head.

"Please help me. Those damn drunken Indians came back and did this." As he spoke blood ran from the corner of his mouth, the bullet must have hit the lower part of his lung. Luta heard movement in the wagon and looking toward the back he saw two young Indian girls tied hand and foot with gags in the mouths. "I gave them the whiskey they wanted…." He was choking on blood unable to breathe. He coughed and spit up more blood. "Damn Crow." These were his last understandable words….he continued to make sounds as his lungs filled with blood and he lost consciousness.

Luta climbed into the wagon and with his knife cut the rope on the hands and feet of the two young girls. They couldn't be more then fourteen if that old. They both reached around their head and untied the gag in their mouth. Neither of them spoke. Both looked at Luta wondering if he were a friend or foe.

Remembering some of the Cheyenne language his mother had taught him, he said. "I am Luta, friend." Neither of them spoke or moved. "Where is your home?" He asked but neither of them showed any expression that they understood any of what he said. "I am Cheyenne, are you Crow?" Again nothing, it was as if they were frozen and could not speak or show any expression.

He found a pick axe and shovel on the wagon so he dug a couple of shallow graves and buried the two men. He took the harness off the dead mule threw a rope on his hind leg and with it wrapped around his saddle horn he pulled the mule off and out of the way.

He stripped the saddle off Lucky and put it in the wagon. He adjusted the harness a little and put it on Lucky. Lucky was not happy and to show it he made a weak attempt to kick Luta a couple times. Lucky had never been under harness so it took a while for him to get the hang of it. Luta wanted to get a few miles from the dead mule as he knew it would bring wolves and maybe a bear during the night. He found what he was looking for.

Photo by Rachel Rosenboom

A nice camp site by a crooked rushing river. The two girls were still huddled in the back of the wagon. Neither of them had spoken a word or shown any expression that they understood anything Luta had said. Luta did his best to pay them no attention as he went about the business of setting up camp. Hoping this would give them a sense of freedom.

Lucky was glad to get the harness off and to show Luta how he felt. He found a nice spot and rolled on his back. He got to his feet and shook as if to shake off any sign of that harness.

Luta found a fish pole and some tackle in the wagon and went to the stream to see if he could catch supper. He said nothing to the girls and had his back to them so if they wanted to escape they could. He had good luck fishing and caught three fish twelve to fourteen inches in length that would be more than enough for the three of them. He cleaned the fish, got them frying and then opened a can of beans. Once the fish were crisp and the beans hot, he dished up three tin plates and placed two of them on the wagon seat with a spoon in each. He took his food down by the stream and sat on a log to enjoy the meal.

When he finished he went back to the wagon and noted that the fish were gone but the beans were not touched. He took the coffee pot down to the stream and filled it with fresh water to make coffee in the morning. The sun was already setting in the west. He washed the dishes, cleaned the skillet and got his bedroll. With his Winchester he crawled under the wagon, it had been a long day. There were several cases of whiskey in the wagon but he had not drank any of it. He was not feeling guilty or sorry for himself and he wondered if that made a difference.

He was still thinking about how he felt as he made himself comfortable. He had to admit that he liked the warm feeling of the whiskey going down and the burning of it. When he was alone after the killing he felt the need for the whiskey. But the impact of the events with the Crow and seeing how quick life can leave a body, the fact that the fate of these two young girls depended on him gave his life new meaning.

CHAPTER TWENTY-TWO

"What you do with us?" The small voice spoke English with an accent but she was easy to understand.

"I am taking you to Wind River the Arapahoe reservation." Luta was eating some bacon and having a cup of coffee. He had placed a plate of bacon for them on the wagon seat.

"No! We no go there." Her voice was louder, stronger.

"Why? Is that not where your family is?"

"We spoiled, damaged. We disgrace to father. We no go there." This was the first time she was almost out of the wagon. Luta had seen them sneak out when nature called and they didn't think he would notice but this was the first time either of them had spoken.

"I don't understand. You have done nothing, why do you think this?" He got to his feet and was facing the young girl who was leaning over the wagon seat. Her sister was almost hidden behind her.

"The Crow take, we sold to white man and you bring back. No one believe we no damaged." She was almost screaming the words at him.

"Where do you want me to take you?" He was pouring himself more coffee. He got another tin cup and poured them a cup. "Would you like some coffee?"

"Do not know coffee." She took the tin cup and looked inside. "Dirty hot water?"

Luta laughed as he was taking a sip and almost choked. "Just take a sip, like this." He took a sip from his cup.

She just held the cup and looked at him. "Where you go?"

"I am going to a place high in the mountains. I will stay there all winter. Just a few men and only two women live there. It is not a very nice place"

She looked at him and then at the coffee, she watched him sip on the coffee. After a while she took a small sip and made a face. She turned, speaking Arapahoe, handed it to her sister. They disappeared behind the wagon flap.

He finished his coffee, cleaned up the dishes and put out the fire with the remaining coffee. He hitched the team and was climbing onto the wagon when she poked her head out.

"We go where you go for winter." Before he could say anything she disappeared back into the wagon.

He turned on the seat, pulled the flap back and said, "No, I do not think that is a good idea. We will have to come up with a better plan." He flipped the reins over the backs of the team and said, "Giddy up." Lucky was doing better but was still not happy to be hitched. Luta spent the whole morning thinking about what to do with the girls. He felt that Wind River would be the best place for them but they sounded determined not to go back there. He had not come up with a solution when about noon he saw a circle of oaks up ahead which meant there was water.

He found a spring coming out of some rocks and a nice place to let Lucky and the Jenny graze. He had no more than pulled the team to a halt when the girls jumped out of the back of the wagon. By the time he had the team unhitched, watered and grazing the girls had built a fire ring of rocks, gathered some small twigs, dry leaves and larger wood. They were ready for him to put his back to the wind, cup his hands and put a match to the dry leaves and small twigs in the center of the rocks. They quickly made a tepee of larger wood to make a good cooking fire.

One of them had gathered some acorns while the other got the skillet hot and some meat pounded to make it tender and ready to cook. By the time the meat had a good sear on one side they had removed the acorn meat from the shells and laid them on the meat. When the meat was done they took the acorns and put them on a rock to cool. Later they would grind them and mix with flour to make fry bread.

Luta had to admit the meat seemed to be tender and the acorns added to the flavor. Later that afternoon he came to a small town. There was a general store so he stopped in front to go in a buy some supplies. He told the girls it would be best if they were not seen by anyone. He got a sack of flour, a sack of rice and another of potatoes. He got some coffee, salt, sugar and a tin of pepper. He found some canned peaches and a slab of bacon. He got the girls each a pair of ladies cotton union suits for twenty cents each and a pair of wool hose that came up over the knee for sixteen cents each. A pair of boy's wool mittens for ten cents each and a red corduroy sheep lined coat with a sheep lined collar for three dollars each. He got himself a pair of wool gloves for twenty-two cents and a pair of heavy lumbermen's wool socks for twenty cents.

Thinking about building a cabin, Luta got a roll of tar paper, one hundred foot by three feet for $3.60, a gallon of pine tar for forty cents and two window screens and greased paper for twenty cents each. He would like to have glass but they didn't have any. He found a box of roofing nails for fifteen cents and a box of 16 penny nails for twenty cents. On his way to the register he saw a game of checkers for a quarter so he picked it up.

There was already supplies in the wagon, a sack of beans, some canned goods, a little coffee, flour, sugar and some spices. Dr. Richard had several blankets and a big horse hide rug that he had on the floor of the area in the wagon were he slept. He had clothes, a scatter gun, a revolver, tools and several cases of whiskey.

The man totaled Luta's things and it came to fourteen dollars and seventy-five cents. Luta gave him fifteen dollars and told him to give him the change in rock candy. He loaded all the supplies in the wagon and they were on their way. That night after supper Luta gave the girls their things and they had to hurry into the wagon to try them on. It was the first union suits they had ever seen but it didn't take them long to figure out how to wear them. The coats were a little big for them but that was better than being a little small. They came out by the fire all dressed for cold weather.

Luta gave each of them a piece of rock candy. They looked at it and then at Luta not knowing what it was or what to do with it. Luta took a piece and put it in his mouth. "Just suck on it. Let it melt in your mouth."

After a few seconds, what they thought of the rock candy showed on their faces. They both had big smiles as they rolled the candy around in their mouths. They were beginning to be more relaxed around Luta, fear was replaced with trust. They had never had clothes with buttons but they learned fast how to use them. They liked the feel of the store brought clothes and their smell.

Without really coming to a decision, Luta had made a decision.

CHAPTER TWENTY-THREE

Luta gave the signal, three shots, two as fast as could be fired and the third five seconds later. Going up the steep incline Luta had to lead the team. The trail winds upward over loose rocks to the top of the red wall. Lucky and Jenny had to strain to pull the big wagon. It was slow going but with Luta pulling on them and encouraging them, the team made it to the top.

Slim Alexander was seated on the slab of white rock watching. Adam Alexander was about thirty, and thin as a rail. He had a scar under his right eye, a burn from a branding iron when a calf came untied, kicked and it burned him. He was tall, five feet ten or eleven inches but didn't weigh more than a hundred and twenty-five pounds.

"Fancy wagon, where did you come by it?" He had a Henry rifle on his lap and a colt single action Peacemaker on his hip.

"The good Doc was killed by some Crow, I got there in time to spoil their fun but not soon enough to save him." Luta was breathing hard from the climb.

"That good Doc have any whiskey to make his snake oil?" Slim was on his feet. "We are starting to run low and Harv has gone to rationing it."

"Yes, I have some. I will talk to Harvey about it."

Luta got back up on the wagon seat and made the sharp turn to the left and down a narrow opening to the grassy green fertile valley. He could see some stolen cattle grazing with several horses. Three log cabins were bunched up by a corral with an outhouse behind them. There was a lean-to type shelter in the corral. He could see Harvey Logan and his woman, a prostitute he had rescued, on the porch of the largest cabin.

As the wagon rumbled into the yard, Lonny Logan and his wife came out of the next cabin. Lonny was Harvey's younger brother, a strong man, five foot eight to ten inches and weighting one eighty or one ninety. He had auburn hair and a mustache. His wife was a chubby gal with dish water blond hair and a quick temper.

Luta stopped the wagon in front of Harvey's cabin. As always Harvey was dressed in a dark black suit, dirty white shirt and black tie. His woman was tall, almost as tall as Harvey who was five eight. She was Irish and had red hair but not the quick temper. In fact she was always very calm and congenial.

Luta explained to them how he came upon the wagon and its contents. He told them he wanted to spend the winter and that he wanted to get started on a cabin. When he was here the last time he shared the third cabin with Slim but he did not want to do that. That cabin was set up with six bunks, three double bunks and any guests that came, stayed in it.

Slim rode up, they didn't keep a lookout all the time. If they heard the signal, one of them would go check. They would keep a man up there for a week or two after they pulled a job. Most of the local law enforcement knew it was suicide to try to get in so they did not even make an attempt.

Luta had just introduced Bina and Aamu. They were very shyly peeping their heads out of the wagon flap.

"Whiskey and poontang, damn man you…." Luta interrupted Slim and the look on his face and in his eyes could not be misunderstood.

"Slim! You are not to touch either of these girls."

"You bring two young Injuns in here and then won't share. Damn man, I guess I could give you a couple bucks."

"They are not for sale and they are not to be touched or you will answer to Mr. Winchester." They had never seen Luta this way, in fact no one had but his anger and determination could not be mistaken.

"Okay, we all know the rules. No one touches anything that doesn't belong to them." Harvey had stood up and was at the edge of the porch.

"Park your wagon over on the other side of the corral. I will come talk to you about the whiskey later. Lonny and I have been planning a job, we need one before winter sets in."

Luta flicked the reins and the odd team put the wagon into motion. He parked it east and west so that the north wind wouldn't blow in. The bluff protected it from the east wind and the lean-to a little from the west. It was not a prefect set up but the best he could do. Just to the north of the wagon was where he wanted to build his cabin. There was a good supply of aspen and ponderosa pine nearby. Some of them were dead and these were the ones he wanted to use as they would not shrink and leave slots for the wind to blow in.

He put the jenny in the corral and turned Lucky loose. He would use the mule to drag the logs down. There were plenty of good tools in the wagon and he wanted to get started the first thing in the morning. He would sleep in the lean-to until he got at least the shell of his cabin built. It was not good but he thought it was better than sharing the cabin with Slim. This way he would be between the girls and Slim. He didn't worry about Harvey or Lonny as their women would kill them if they tried anything.

Bina and Aamu were far better help then Luta ever dreamed they would be. They were strong and learned quickly. The first step was to build a stone and rock foundation to keep the logs off of the ground and prevent rot. They used the team and wagon to haul material to the building site. Once the foundation was in place, they began to haul logs. It wasn't long and the two girls were falling trees with the two man saw. In this case, the two girl saw. The logs were notched in the top and bottom of each end. Then they were stacked to form walls. With the two girls on one end of a log and Luta on the other they lifted them into place. After the logs were stacked, gaps remained in places. These were filled with a dirt, sand, and water mixture that when dried was almost like stone. They also used the pine tar mixed with wood chips. Luta saved out some of the best rocks when building the foundation to use for a fireplace and chimney. The cabin was ten by twenty feet and would have a loft for the girls to sleep in.

The roof would not have much pitch as the gable ends of the cabin were only a few logs tall. This did not allow much room for the loft so Luta made the walls a couple logs higher and put cross beams in at about the five foot mark to support the loft. His bunk would be under the loft. Flat lumber was difficult to come by so Luta made the decision to use the wagon to build a door, the floor of the loft, shutters for the two windows, his bunk, a table and a counter to prepare food. He had to use leather for hinges for the door and shutters. He used part of the canvas from the wagon to make a sling bunk bed. The mattress pad from the wagon fit well in the loft for the girls.

The two windows were thirty inches square. That was the size of the window screen and the greased paper. He used some flat lumber from the wagon to frame up the door and windows. Both windows were on the south wall so they had good sun light when the shutters were open.

They worked from sun up to sun down as the days were getting shorter, the nights were getting colder and the first snow would not be too far in the future. Harvey, Lonny and Slim were planning a job. They had plenty of cattle so rustling was out, as it was too risky trying to sell stolen cattle. They went back and forth on a bank or a train. They asked Luta to join them in Harvey's cabin one evening.

"A bank is more dangerous because in these small towns the town marshal is only a few doors away and there is often a tavern right across the street with men and guns. You have to rob it during banking hours. I think a train is better." Luta was having a glass of whiskey. He had to admit he liked the feel of it going down. He limited himself to just one glass a night, the last thing he wanted was to not be in control.

"Lots of rich folks on them trains, could get all kinds of stuff from them." Slim rubbed his hands together with the thought of it.

"I don't want any part of robbing the passenger cars." Luta surprised them with this statement.

"Why? Looks like easy picking to me."

"Again, too many men with guns. You turn your back and you're dead. I would find a steep grade like the one just south of Casper where the engine has to really work to pull the train up the slope. I would grease the rails with bear grease and when it slows down, jump on and uncouple the passenger cars from the mail car and engine. Let them roll back down the hill so we don't have to worry about their guns. We take the money in the mail car and we are gone." Luta took a sip of his whiskey and waited for their questions or comments.

"I like that idea, we had bullets flying all around us when we rode out of Horse Creek." Lonny looked to his brother to see what he thought.

"We have to have more information and we need it fast, as snow will be flying one of these days. Lonny, you and Slim go and check the train schedules, check out that hill south of Casper. We need to know if there are trees or brush to hide our horses. Find the best and fastest way back here. See if there is a good place to ride east and then swing around west. We also need some supplies for the winter. We want to get the supplies before we pull a job. Have the women make a list and take a couple pack horses with you." Harvey refilled his glass with whiskey.

They talked of what they would need. "We will need an axe to break down the door and knock the padlock off the Wells Fargo box."

"What about dynamite?" Slim asked.

"I don't think we will need it and if we were to use it, the whole train would know a robbery was taking place. That would mean the train crew and others with guns. If we do this right I think we can get the job done without anyone knowing about it until it is too late to stop us." Luta looked at the others for reaction to what he said.

"I agree, no dynamite. Let's get more information and then make the final plans." Harvey stood up as if to say the meeting was over.

CHAPTER TWENTY-FOUR

The train was scheduled to get into Casper at six A.M. and the steep grade was about a half hour south of Casper. So they figured most of the passengers would still be sleeping and if they were lucky, some of the train crew.

They were there just before five, greasing the tracks. It was a chilly morning so the bear grease was easy to wipe on the iron rails and it stayed in place. They greased each rail for a distance of about two hundred feet. On the two trains that Lonny and Slim had watched come into Casper, the express/mail car was next to the engine. It had a door in the back of the car and one on each side of the car.

Their plan was for Lonny to bang on the side door while Luta pulled the coupling pin and Harvey with an axebroke down the door at the end of the car. Luta would be right there to follow Harvey into the car. Slim would stay with the horses and bring them up when he saw the side door come open.

Their scheme was going just as planned. When the steam engine hit the bear grease the big driver wheels began to spin. The train had already lost about half its speed and was only going ten to fifteen miles an hour when it hit the grease. With the wheels burning their way down to the iron before it could get traction to inch forward it was almost at a standstill.

Luta pulled the coupling mechanism, the four freight cars, two passenger cars and dining car began to roll back down the grade. Lonny was banging on the door with a club and Harvey with just two blows of the axe and the door was open. The engineer and fireman were both looking out their windows to see what the problem was. Neither noticed the noise or the loss of seven cars. The messenger in the express/mail car, who had been sleeping. Was just putting a match to the oil lantern hanging over the desk.

Harvey rushed into the car with his colt in one hand and the axe in the other. Luta was right behind him. The messenger started to go for a revolver on the desk but a loud, "Don't try it!" from Harvey stopped his hand in midair. "Down on your belly, hands behind your back!" The messenger looked at the colt in Harvey's hand, did not hesitate to drop to the floor.

The Wells Fargo wood and metal strong box with a big padlock was next to the desk. With one swing of his axe Harvey broke off the heavy padlock. Luta opened the side door for Lonny to jump in and to give Slim the signal to bring up the horses. Inside the strong box were two leather pouches. One lettered for the Casper State Bank and the other for the First Bank of Buffalo. Harvey picked up both pouches, Luta grabbed the revolver off the desk and the rifle off the wall over the desk.

Harvey handed Lonny the axe, holstered his colt and with the two mail pouches jumped on the back of his horse. Luta noticed a parcel of books tied with string as he was turning to leave. He seized them by the top string with the hand holding the revolver and took them with him. The train had lost all its forward motion and it wasn't until just then that the engineer and fireman realized what was happening. Luta and Lonny jumped on their horses and the four train robbers rode off into the early morning darkness. They had not fired a shot or had a shot fired at them. On their scouting trip Lonny and Slim had found a small shallow stream about a half mile east of the tracks that ran from the northwest to the southeast. They rode to it and then rode up stream in the water to cover any tracks. About a half mile up stream they came to a cattle crossing with all kinds of tracks and rode out of the stream. They turned west and rode hard to get across the railroad tracks before the train got there. The train had to back up, hook up to the cars and go back up the grade. There was still some grease on the driver wheels and on the track so it took the train forever to top the grade and get up to speed. By this time the robbers were several miles west headed for the Hole in the Wall.

In Harvey's cabin with a glass of whiskey in their hands to celebrate, they broke the small lock on the pouches and dumped there contenents on the table. Each pouch had one hundred George Washington dollar bills with a paper band around them, fifty two dollar bills with Jefferson on them, fifty Benjamin Franklin fifty dollar notes, one hundred five dollar notes with Andrew Jackson on them and a pack of fifty twenty dollar notes with Hamilton on them. The pouch for Casper also had a pack of fifty ten dollar notes with a portrait of Robert Morris on them. The total take was eight thousand nine hundred dollars or two thousand, two hundred and twenty-five dollars for each of them.

The best part was, the bills came from the Bank of Kansas City and they were not new bills. The serial numbers were not in sequence. They could not be traced back to the train robbery. As long as none of them got crazy throwing money around they were in the clear. The best part was they all planned to spend the winter right there in the Hole in the Wall so none of the money would be spent until next spring. Six months from now the train robbery would be old news.

"This calls for a toast. Ladies, you gals get a glass to join us?" The women were watching with interest and giddy with delight. "Here's to the Logan gang. May they continue to prosper." Harvey was, as always, dressed in his dark suit with a white shirt and tie. He looked like he could be a successful businessman toasting his workers.

"We don't have any need for this money until next spring. So to get rid of any temptation to ride out of here or to get in a big money poker game this winter, I will keep this for us until the pass is open next spring." Harvey was putting the money back into the pouches.

"No! That's not right. I want mine to count and keep." Slim slammed his whiskey glass on the table splashing a little on his hand.

"Too much money, whiskey, a poker game and somebody ends up getting shot. You all know my word is good as gold. I give you my word you can have your share when the pass opens in the spring." Harvey put the bills back in the pouches.

"You guys all got women, I am alone. I wasn't planning on spending the winter in this Hell Hole. I want my share so I can ride." Slim was holding out his hand to Harvey.

"That's what I was afraid of. That is the reason I am keeping the take." Harvey had both pouches in his left hand, his right hand just above the butt of his colt on his hip.

"What the Hell good is it to have money if you can't spend it? We didn't make any agreement to do this." He followed this with a spew of profanities.

"Yes, we did. We agreed to make one heist before the snow came. You even went and helped Lonny get supplies for the winter."

"I think we should at least vote on it. Lonny? Luta? What do you guys think of Harvey keeping all our money?"

"I have no problem with it. If I don't have it in my cabin I don't have to worry about it. I wasn't planning on going anywhere until next spring. I just got my cabin built." Luta took the last sip of his whiskey and set the glass on the table.

"Slim. It is best this way. You will have more money next spring than you have ever had in your life. You can dream all winter about what you are going to buy. You get your share now and ride and it will be gone by next spring or even worse it will be gone and you will be in jail." Lonny set his glass on the table and motioned for his wife to come.

"I ain't stupid. I ain't about to show a wad of bills to anyone."

"By next spring this will have blown over. Right now every law man in the territory is looking at anyone spending money. Like you say, what good is it if you can't spend it? You sleep on this Slim and you will know that I am right." Harvey's hand was still poised over his colt.

Luta started for the door. "It was good, better than I thought it would be. Nice take and no shots fired."

"Yeah, the bank job got us a total of eight hundred and we had bullets flying all around us, one of us could have been hit or killed." Lonny had his hand on the door latch.

"I ain't happy Harv, I will sleep on it but I don't think I will change my mind." Slim downed the last of his whiskey in a gulp and slammed the glass down on the table. He left a trail of profanities behind him as he walked out and slammed the cabin door.

CHAPTER TWENTY-FIVE

The first snow came like a big fluffy blanket over the Wyoming valley. Several inches of big flakes floated down all day to make the land between the mountain ranges look white and pure. The next morning, rabbits had made tracks in the white blanket.

Photo by Rachel Rosenboom

The girls made some rabbit snares using rope and a bent tree branch. They made several as the more snares the better their chance of catching a meal. Not only did the girls know several ways to cook the rabbit, they also knew several ways to use the fur.

Luta was pleased with the books he got off the train. Five in total, The Jumping Frog of Calaveras County by Mark Twain, Great Expectations by Charles Dickens, The Three Musketeers by Alexandre Dumas, Moby-Dick by Herman Melville and Roughing It by Mark Twain. It was Roughing It by Mark Twain that Luta kept going back to and reading it again and again. These books played a major role in Luta's decision and helped the girls to their decision.

Photo by Ken Wilbur, edited by my son Brent

Once the first snow came to the Hole in the Wall, it wasn't long and the pass was closed for the winter. It was a hard winter, the snow was hard-packed and with snowshoes it was easy to walk on. Luta made a sled out of some of the flat boards from the wagon and this made bringing in large game rather easy. The girls showed him how they would cross the ice and bust up the beaver lodges to get the valuable skins. They also showed him how to build a scaffold to keep the venison secure from the wolves. They never had a single complaint about the cold winter weather. In fact, they seemed to be good-hearted and full of fun.

They would read the books together out loud in English and then discuss the paragraph in Arapahoe. They were rather loud and at first it was disturbing to Luta but they did it with such joy and laughter that he came to take pleasure in hearing them. The good doctor had a couple nice coal oil lanterns in his wagon and enough coal oil to last all winter. He also had a large mirror that fit behind the lantern that gave off a beam of light.

When the girls were in a real silly, giggy mood, they would get into the doctor's trunk of clothes and play dress up. The first time Luta saw this he had told them he was going to see if he could get a deer, so they thought he would be gone several hours. But when Luta was leaving he noticed Slim standing on his porch watching him pull the sled into the trees. He did an about face and returned to the cabin. He could hear them giggle and laugh before he got to the door. They were surprised to see him but were relieved when he laughed and did not show any anger.

Photo by Ken Wilbur, photo edited by my son Brent

That was when he decided they needed to learn to handle the doctor's revolver. It was a five-shot Colt Paterson revolver model with a long nine inch barrel. It was a .36 caliber and with the long barrel was effective as many rifles at one hundred yards. It was heavy but the girls were strong and proved to be able to handle the weapon. Aamu was the most accurate but Bina could get off the second shot faster. If the target was the size of a man, both shots could be fatal.

The target practice did not go unnoticed and this pleased Luta. He wanted Slim to observe how well the girls could handle the revolver. He made it a point one day when talking with Lonny when Slim was within hearing distance, to tell him that whenever they went out they took the Paterson and when he was gone and they were in the cabin alone, they had it handy.

Both the girls and Luta enjoyed reading but when they started to get cabin fever they could always go hunting. The girls would take the Paterson and go rabbit hunting. Luta took his Winchester and looked for bigger game.

The girls had trapped a couple beaver and were getting the pelts ready so they could make some warm winter caps. Some days the wind would blow the snow off the mountains down through the valley and it was dangerous to be far from the cabin as you could get lost in the blinding snow. These were the days they would stay in the cabin and read or play checkers. Luta had taught them the game and they were very competitive. Once in a while the game would end with one of them knocking the board to the floor and running to the loft in frustration.

One windy snowy winter day when it was too nasty to be outside they were all in the cabin reading. Luta noticed that they were having a disagreement. At first he didn't pay much attention but it continued and they got louder and they sounded angry. They were speaking their native tongue so he could not understand but he could tell they were both getting worked up about something.

"What's your problem girls?" They both stopped talking and came over to where he was seated. The girls had the spring seat from the wagon in the cabin with the horse hide rug over it. It was Luta's favorite place to sit.

"White man's words say if you don't like you that nobody like you." Bina held out the book they were reading. "I think that true."

"He also say you have to challenge yourself on how you like yourself. What mean this challenge?" Aaum was pointing at the book Bina was holding. "Challenge mean to fight, how can you fight yourself? The book is no tail it is all bull." Aaum was so upset she was speaking half English and half Arapahoe.

Luta had never seen them like this. He could tell it was very important to them so he put down his book and did his best to make some sense of what they were in disagreement about.

"He say you have to enjoy the journey. You have to enjoy each day. I think that true." Bina kept pointing to the book.

"It is a smelly pile of garbage. All I have to do is like myself, like to travel with myself and everyone will like me?" Aaum threw up her hands and shook her head.

Luta wanted to laugh at them but he could see how serious they both were and that this was not a time to smile, say nothing of laughing. He stood up and took hold of a hand of each. "This is what is so great about books, readers do not always agree on what it means or what the author is saying. You could both be correct, it means different things to different people. The author just wants you to think about it and make up your own mind." He spoke in a soft voice, hoping to calm them down.

"If you don't like yourself, how can I like you?" Bina had calmed down a little, her voice was not as loud as it had been.

Aaum had to stop and think. She also had calmed down now that Luta was holding her hand. "That seem too easy, too simple. Life is not simple."

"Everything in books is not always correct, it is just the author's opinion." In his attempt to explain it to the girls Luta was learning as much as he was teaching.

"If you do not enjoy the day, you are not fun to be near. Do you like to be near me when I am angry?" Bina's question made Aaum stop and think.

"No, when you are angry you are…." Aaum finished her sentence in Arapahoe and Luta did not understand but Bina laughed.

"I do not like it much when you laugh at me but I would rather you laugh at me than to be angry with me."

"I was not angry with you, I was angry with the words in the book."

"That is what books can do, books can make us happy, sad or angry. Books can take us on a journey or they can teach us to read. Let's sleep on this, I think it gives us all something to think about." Luta was happy that it seemed to be ending on a happy note.

CHAPTER TWENTY-SIX

It was a hard winter in Colorado. Lots of snow and cold weather. Martha had spent it in Bear Lake and it was a good thing that she did. Sarah and Dusty became the proud parents of a baby boy and she helped the mid-wife deliver the baby and she was there to help Sarah after the birth.

She also spent a great deal of time at the Circle C ranch. She got along very well with Loretta Collins and enjoyed the time they spent together. With the winter being hard the men had to work to make sure the cattle had feed.

Photo by Rachel Rosenboom

Martha also spent a great deal of time with Jesse. If they were not outside they were playing board games such as the Mansion of Happiness which required the players to race around a sixty-six space track with virtues and vices. The goal was to be the first to reach the Mansion of Happiness. Mr. and Mrs. Collins would play with them from time to time. They also played tiddlywinks which was played with small discs called "winks" of different colors. Players used a larger, heavier disc, called a "squidger" to pop a wink into the air by pressing down on one side of the wink. The objective of the game was to get the wink to land inside a small pot in the center of the board or on top of an opponent's wink.

They also spent hours playing Hearts. A card game in which the players aim was to avoid taking tricks that contain hearts or the queen of spades. However, if a player had a good hand of hearts and could take all the tricks with hearts plus the queen of spades, the opponents all got twenty-six penalty points added to their score. These games plus a bowl of hot popcorn and a warm fireplace made great fun on a cold winter night.

It was on one of her visits to the Circle C that Martha happened to see Loretta in her sewing room working on a white satin dress. When she asked her what she was making her reply was, "You never know when you will need something so it is best to be prepared and I enjoy sewing satin. It is so smooth."

Jesse would share his dream of a big horse and cattle ranch with Martha. His parent's ranch ran up against the west end of Bear Lake. He had shown her a spot where he wanted to build a log home on the lake. She liked the idea and offered several suggestions that Jesse agreed to.

The days started to get longer, the sun moved a little to the north each morning and the days did not seem to be as cold. They would get a little melting of snow during the sunny days but it would freeze again during the colder nights.

Dusty and Sarah had their hands full with the store and their young family so they were glad to have Martha to help out. Martha enjoyed both the work in the store and helping with the housework and children. She told Sarah about Jesse's dream to build a log home on the lake.

"Is that your dream too?"

"Jesse is a good man and I know that he loves me. I saw his mother working on a white satin dress and when I asked her about it she said she just liked to work with satin and it was always good to be prepared. I think Jesse is going to ask me to marry him." She said with a giggle as she picked up the baby who was fussing. It was time for a diaper change.

"That would be awesome having you right across the lake."

"Yes and not too far from the folks. It is a dream come true." Martha took off the dirty diaper and put some powder on his little bottom. She put on a clean diaper and put her hand under the diaper so as not to stick him with the pin. She always worried that she would nick him or that the safety pin would come undone. She picked him up and put him on her shoulder. He was such a good baby always laughing. Sarah said that was because he was just like his dad, full of gas. Martha liked to be around Sarah and Dusty. They teased each other but it was easy to see they also loved each other. Dusty was such a big bear of a man, yet he could be so gentle, so thoughtful.

Martha knew marriage was not always fun and games. The pleasure seemed to be in the people not in what they had. It was rare, growing up that she heard her parents angry with each other. When they did, neither of them called names or was physical. Her mother would worry and be upset when her dad was not around but when he was there she was most always in a good mood.

She couldn't help but wonder what her marriage would be like. Would she be a good wife, a good mother? She knew it was easy to dwell on everything that was wrong opposed to everything that was right or good. She could see that daily life in a marriage was of the ordinary not of the spectacular. She knew she had to find happiness in the routines of a home, her question was could she do that?

CHAPTER TWENTY-SEVEN

Luta had gone hunting and Beni had taken the revolver and went to check their snare traps. She wanted to make some rabbit eggs. She would cut a piece of rabbit meat about the size of a chicken egg, rub salt and pepper into it, wrap some bacon or pork belly around it and fry it in bear grease.

Slim saw them both leave, he had been waiting weeks for this chance. He snuck around the Corral and came up on the blind side of the cabin. He caught Aamu by surprise and had her pushed up against the horse hide spring seat before she could react. She fought and he hit her on the right side of her face. She continued to fight him and he hit her again this time on her left eye brow. The second blow dazed her and she went limp in his grasp. He unbuckled his belt and let his pants fall to his ankles. He ripped at her clothes and was so intent on what he was doing that he didn't hear the cabin door open.

Beni came in with two rabbits in one hand and the colt revolver in the other. She saw what was about to happen and reacted. The .36 caliber slug hit Slim in the back of his head and the force of the shot slammed him forward. Aamu had come to and with all the strength she could muster shoved him off her. His arms flung wildly as he rolled to the cabin floor.

Harvey had heard the shot and came running to see what was going on. He got to the open cabin door to see Beni still holding the Paterson and Aamu covered with blood on the horsehide seat. Both of the girls seemed to be in shock, neither of them were crying or saying anything.

Slim was taking his last gasping breath as he lay on the floor with his pants down around his ankles.

By the time Luta returned Slim was wrapped in his bedroll and up on the scaffold beside the cabin where he would stay until it was possible for them to dig a grave. Lonny and his wife had come to help clean up. The cabin was clean and Aamu was patched up. She had a cut on her right cheek bone and another on her left eye brow. Both areas bleed greatly so it looked worse when Harvey first saw her than it turned out to be. The girls were both in the loft still sobbing.

"Check on the girls, Luta, and then come over to my cabin."

Luta went to see if he could console the girls. He didn't say anything, he just laid a hand on each of their shoulders. They were weeping but they had run out of tears. At times it was more of a whimper, a sob of mourning more than crying. Aamu's face had some swelling and she would have a couple black eyes.

Later in Harvey's cabin they talked about what had happened. "Well. We all know the rules. We are our own law, judge and jury. No one is to touch anything that doesn't belong to them. Slim was warned. It looks to me like Beni shot a train robber that was doing wrong and so she and her sister are entitled to his share as their reward. Do you guys agree or disagree?"

Luta and Lonny looked at each other but neither said anything. Harvey's solution to the problem came as a surprise to both of them. Lonny was the first to gain his voice, "If that is okay with you guys I am fine with it."

"We will have to come up with a story about how the girls came about the money. We will also have to figure what they can do with it so that it doesn't come back on you guys. That is a huge amount of money for two Indian girls to have. For that matter it is a huge amount for anyone to have." Luta was thinking that even a train robber could be an honest man. Without hesitation standing up for his own interpretation of what was right and wrong.

"Yes for now just tell them that they are not in any trouble and that they will get some money as they stopped Slim from doing something very wrong. Don't tell them how much." Harvey reached for the whiskey bottle to refill his glass.

"Luta what are your plans when it warms up and the pass is open?" Lonny held his glass out to Harvey and he poured him a drink.

"I have been reading about California and I plan to take the train out there and start a new life. I am going to leave Luta in Colorado and become Lou Schroeder. I don't know if I will start a horse ranch or what but I will have enough money to do just about anything I want. I learned on this train robbery that I was not a good man for the job. When the messenger saw us and started for his gun.....I don't think I could or would have shot him. Had he not stopped when you yelled at him Harv, he could have killed you."

"We don't always know what we will do in a situation. You had no trouble reacting to that cowhand in the poker game. I knew from the first time we talked that you were not a cold blooded killer but you did help plan a successful train robbery. I saw your face and eyes when you warned Slim about the Injun gals and I think he would be in the same place he is if Beni had not done him in first." Harvey took a sip of his whiskey.

"I would ride the river with you anytime and have faith that you would have my back." Lonny took a small drink of his whiskey and let it slush around in his mouth before swallowing it.

"Thanks. I am grateful that you both see this the way you do. Some guys would look at it like Slim did and think he was doing nothing wrong, that they were just savages to be used. I will go talk to the girls and between us maybe we can come up with a plan."

Luta went to the cabin to explain to the girls what the three of them had decided. He knew it would take a while for them to get over this ordeal but time does have a way of healing. If not healing at least allowing people to move on. He was finding that to be true in his case. He had wants, dreams and desires for the first time in months. The books had helped him to come to a decision but today was the first time he was able to express it to anyone, even to himself. When Harvey asked the question it just seemed to roll out and he was surprised at what he was saying.

He would need to spend some time talking to the girls. Telling them his plans. He could not take them with him and he couldn't leave them here. He had noticed them changing, gaining more confidence. They seemed to value themselves more than they did a few months ago. He couldn't help but wonder how this would affect them.

As he walked into the cabin they both turned to look at him with a questioning look on their faces. It was Beni that spoke. "What they do to us?"

"Harvey, Lonny and I all agree that Slim did a very wrong thing and you did the right thing. Harvey said you should get a reward."

"What this reward?" Beni said with a worried look on her face.

"Money. You will get some money, wampum to buy things you want." Luta rubbed his fingers together.

"We get money for killing Slim?" They both had this unbelievable look on their faces, like they could not believe what they were hearing.

"Yes, Slim was an outlaw and the white man gives a reward to those that kill an outlaw or bring them in to the Sheriff."

"How much we get?" The wide-eyed nervous look of worry was turning into smiles.

"Enough to buy many things. You will have to talk about what you would like to buy."

The girls ran to the loft giggling in a silly, high-pitched way. One of them would say something in their native tongue and they both would giggle in short, spasmodic sounds. Luta could not believe that these were the same two that looked stunned with fear when he walked in. What a huge change some good news could make.

Change. Seems as if most everybody goes through something that changes them. Once changed they can never go back to the person they were. They can only hope that the new person is a better person.

CHAPTER TWENTY-EIGHT

"What would you think of us making Adam Alexander a rich, eccentric rancher?" Luta looked to Harvey and Lonny for their thoughts.

"Slim, rich, eccentric? I am not even sure what eccentric means but I don't think Slim was it." Lonny said with a big smile.

"How would that help?" Harvey asked in a puzzled tone.

"Well, we could make up a story of how the girls saved his life in a blizzard and he wanted to repay them."

"How did the girls get to a spot to save his life?" Lonny got up to get a bottle of whiskey and some glasses.

"He could have bought them from this snake oil peddler." Harvey took a glass of whiskey from Lonny.

"They have fallen in love with books and want to buy some books and take them to Wind River, they have a dream of teaching the young to read and loaning the books to the people." Luta took a glass of whiskey from Lonny.

"You mean start a library in the Indian Reservation?" Harvey reached for a glass of whiskey and took a sip. "They have enough money to do it but I don't see the Indian Agent or the elders letting them do it. They will cheat or trick them out of their money."

"I agree. That is why I thought if we made slim into a rich, eccentric man, who had his lawyer go to the banker in Horse Creek and made the banker the manager of their affairs that it could work."

"Where you going to get this lawyer?"

"I would have to be the lawyer." Luta took a sip of whiskey.

Harvey was laughing, "A bank robber is going back into the bank and ask the banker to manage money for two Indian girls?" Now they were all three laughing. "That is so crazy, that it just might work. You would have to get some new clothes, look the part." He was still laughing and so was Lonny and Luta.

"It was different in the book, it wasn't Indian girls and the guy hadn't just robbed the bank a year before but I read about it in one of the books. This guy had the banker take care of some money for this widow. He told the banker he would be back once a year to check the books. He never went back but the banker was always expecting him to. He would even send the banker one of those telegrams from time to time."

"Him not being a bank robber and the widow not being two Indian gals could make a difference." Again, Harvey laughed in a very undignified way and the others joined in.

"Yes, I agree that does make a difference." Luta was laughing because Harvey was making them all laugh.

They didn't get much more done. One of them would say something that made the other two laugh. It wasn't until a couple days later that they made some headway.

"There is no way he could recognize you as one of the bank robbers. You had your face covered and with new clothes and this crazy scheme you won't have anything to worry about. The worst thing that could happen is he would say he wasn't interested. But you know how bankers like money, so I don't see that happening." Harvey was beginning to like the idea. "You got to sell the banker on the idea that Adam Alexander is odd and peculiar. He has more money than Carter has them little liver pills and that in the future he may want to give the banker some more money to do his wishes." *

"The girls have been making plans. They would like to help their people. Their dream is to write a book about their people."

*Dr. Samuel J. Carter a druggist in Erie, Pa. developed the Liver Pills in 1870. The pills were touted to cure headache, constipation, bad digestion, stomach pains and excessive flatulence.

It won't be long and the pass will be open, the days are getting longer and the sun is coming farther north all the time. I have had cabin fever the last few weeks. I am ready to take my gal and go spend a little money. Not so much as to draw attention but enough to make my gal happy." Harvey put his arm around the tall red head.

"Me and my wife want to get out of here for a spell too, it has been a long winter waiting to live it up a little." Lonny and Harvey were so different, sometimes it was hard to believe they were brothers."

Photo by Rachel Rosenboom

"We need to go different directions when we leave here. I have been thinking about it. Some lawman may just be waiting for the pass to open too. I think we best leave in the dark of night.

The snow was almost all melted off the pine trees, Luta had seen ducks and geese flying north, wild flowers were starting to bloom, the pass would be open soon.

They had already been working on a grave for Slim. It was still very hard to dig but with the pick they could go down a ways and then let the sun do its thing and dig a little deeper each day.

Luta and the girls had gone over the plan many times. He had coached them on what to say and what not to say. The girls were excited to get back with their people and to do it not feeling like damaged goods. It was very important to them to make their father proud of them to be of value to the tribe.

Their father had always wanted a son. A young warrior. Their only brother had died at a young age from the white man's fever. This had been a very difficult time for their father and there was nothing that they could do. They hoped that the Library would make him proud of his daughters.

CHAPTER TWENTY-NINE

Luta was waiting when the proprietor opened the doors of his store. Riding out in the middle of the night, Luta on Lucky, Aamu on Slim's horse and Beni on a horse they got from Lonny for the cabin. His wife liked their cabin better than the one they lived in.

"You got up before breakfast didn't ya?" The proprietor was middle aged but looked older, he walked with a limp.

"Yes, on my way to a family get together and need a few things." The girls were waiting in a grove of trees at the edge of town. Luta thought it best that they not come in.

"Well, help yourself and let me know if I can help you find something." He went about his business of opening up for the day.

Luta found a navy blue serge suit with a vest for six dollars that would fit, he also found a white muslin shirt and black string tie for seventy-five cent, a California flannel double breasted twilled blue shirt and a pair of blue York denim pants for seventy-five cents. He found a fine wool fedora with a leather sweatband for forty-five cents. He picked up a pair of cotton summer union suits for the girls, knee length and sleeveless for twenty-five cents each and two boys flannel shirts red and black for twenty-five cents each. They had told him to look for books. He found a McGuffey reader grade level one and another grade level three for twenty cents each and a book by Maurice Thompson, King of Honey Island, the book was leather bound and cost a dollar and five cents. He was on his way to the cash register when he saw a dark brown saddle leather brief case with a price of just two dollars so he added it to the things in his arms.

With the stub of a pencil and a brown paper sack the storekeeper figured up Luta's bill. "It comes to a total of twelve dollars and forty cents." Luta handed him thirteen dollars, got his sixty cents in change and made his way to the door with his arms full.

Luta thought it would be best if he got into his new clothes as soon as possible. If they were to meet anyone it would be easier for them to believe he was a lawyer taking the girls to Wind River. He had never had a suit of clothes so it would be a new experience for him.

That night they camped by a small stream. The girls were still looking at Luta, laughing and talking to each other in Arapahoe. It was later in the evening when they heard a big lobo howling for his mate.

Photo by Paul Rosenboom
(Photo was shot with cell phone through a scope)

It was still rather cold at night so Luta kept getting up every hour or so to feed the fire to give them a little warmth. Hot coffee tasted extra good as Mr. sun was just poking his head up and was not giving off much heat yet. Luta, dressed in his new clothes and wearing his new fedora looked even less like he was half Cheyenne. It was time to replace Luta with Lou.

CHAPTER THIRTY

The banker, Abe Radamaker, took a long draw on his cigar then exhaled audibly. A beefy five-foot-ten, hundred and ninety pounder, he filled the big chair behind the oak desk. His blue eyes scanned the girls and came to rest on Lou.

"Your employer wants me to handle some financial transactions for these two Indian girls?"

"Yes, as I said, the girls were taken from the reservation by a Crow raiding party that traded them to this snake oil peddler for whiskey. The peddler came under hard times and they ended up with my employer Adam Alexander a rich, eccentric rancher. The girls changed his life greatly and my position is to find someone to watch over some money."

"How much money are we talking about?"

"Two-thousand dollars." Ade sat up a little straighter in his chair and took a little more interest.

"You have this money?"

"Yes." Lou patted his brief case.

"What is it that this Mr. Alexander wants done?"

"He wants you to see to the building of a Library and ordering some books."

"On the Indian reservation?"

"Yes, at the edge of Horse Creek so that the white population could take advantage of it if they wish."

"What would the bank get out of this?"

"The bank would get a deposit of two thousand dollars and of course a fee would be paid for the handling of the money." Luta looked like a real tenderfoot in his new clothes as he sat with his knees together and his brief case on his lap.

"Does the Indian agent know of this plan?"

"No, I wanted to speak with you first and deposit the money before I went to the reservation."

Abe leaned back in his big chair and took a long drag on his cigar. This was very out of the ordinary. The more he thought about it the better he liked it. How could the bank not come out ahead? It was his and the banks chance to do something for the town and the reservation, and make money at the same time.

Abe replied. "I think myself and the bank are in a position to help, let me think about this overnight. We can talk in the morning about the details. Would you like to deposit the money for safe keeping?"

"Yes." Lou stood up and followed Abe out of his office to one of the tellers.

"Mr. Fridley, would you take care of this deposit? Mr. Schroeder, I will see you in the morning." He extended his hand to Lou and went back to his office.

Lou took the money out of his case and put it on the counter. The teller counted the money twice and took a pen and deposit ticket from the rack on the counter.

"What is the name on the account?"

"Adam Alexander and/or Lou Schroeder." Lou watched him write out the receipt and open the account.

"Will you and or Mr. Alexander be writing drafts on this account?" He paused and looked up at Lou.

"I am hoping to make a deal with Mr. Radamaker where he will be seeing to that. I will know more when we meet in the morning. I guess for now, I will just deposit the money."

"Very well, you can let me know tomorrow if you will be writing drafts. I will get a copy of your signature at that time." He handed Lou the receipt for the deposit.

The Indian agent, Herman Husker was not sure a Library was a good idea but after Abe Radamaker spoke with him he changed his mind. They found a building spot on the east edge of Horse Creek and Abe hired three local men to build the Library.

Lou wrote letters to his parents and to Squirt telling them what he was doing and what his plans for the future were. He posted them and was reading the local newspaper while he watched the men work on the Library. The two girls came to see how it was going.

"What is that you are reading?" Beni asked.

"It is the local newspaper it comes out once a week and tells the local news and a little bit of national news." Lou folded the paper and handed it to Beni.

Beni spoke to Aamu in Arapahoe while they checked out the newspaper. Lou could see that they were in a deep discussion. "Could we do something like this? With news of the reservation, births, deaths and stories of the elders?"

"I don't know. Guess we could go see the newspaper editor and find out."

At the newspaper office they found Mr. Riser to be very interested. A short man with as much ink on his hands and face as he had on his apron, he spoke with a German accent. "I could print you one page front and back for two cents a copy with a minimum of one hundred copies. I would suggest that we start with a monthly edition."

The girls were excited. Mr. Husker also liked the idea as he could put in things he wanted the tribe to know. Lou talked the girls into making it a free paper and if it went well they could sell advertising to cover the cost. They did not understand advertising and how that worked but Lou did his best to explain it to them. They settled on Wind River Signal as the name. Each month they would have a story from one or two of the elders, the birthdays for that month, any births or deaths and a column by the Indian agent.

Lou waited long enough to see the first edition of the Wind River Signal by co-editors Beni and Aamu. The Library building was almost completed and books had been ordered. The girls had living quarters in the back of the Library, a kitchen with a living area and a bedroom. The girls were already holding reading classes for both children and adults. The total cost for the building and the books came to just over five hundred dollars so they still had a large sum of money in the fund. Lou told Mr. Radamaker that he would be stopping back to check the books.

Good-byes came with tears and hugs from the girls. As Lou mounted Lucky, he also felt strong feelings that he had for these young girls. Lives were changed and lives would continue to change. He felt confident that he was leaving the girls in a better situation than he found them. He even had to admit that it was better that he had not returned them to the reservation when he found them almost a year earlier. So much had happened in that time, so many changes. The books taken from the train robbery had played an important part in both the lives of the girls and in his. His life had gone from bad to worse but he felt good about this new direction it was taking. He was excited about boarding the train to this place the books told him about.

He thought of Slim and the train robbery. Things would not be as they were without the train robbery and Slim. The last second act of picking up the books from the mail car. Slim forcing himself on Aamu. Beni coming to her rescue. Harvey and Lonny giving up Slim's share of the take. All these events played a significant role in their lives. Too often we are ruled by things that are wrong with us opposed to all the things that are right with us. The girls were now in a position to help their tribe, to change lives. This was their chance to make their father proud. This would not have been possible without the bad things they were forced to endure.

CHAPTER THIRTY-ONE

As Lou rode Lucky into Bear Lake early Saturday morning he was in a good mood. Things were going well, he was looking forward to seeing his family and being off on the train to a new adventure in California.

He was surprised when he entered the store expecting to see Sarah or Dusty and instead he saw a man he did not know behind the counter. The man turned and said something to a young lad and the boy hurried out the back door of the store.

"I was looking for Sarah or Dusty?" Lou stopped in front of the man at the cash register.

"They are out at the valley, went last evening. Big wedding out there this weekend. Ms. Martha is getting married." He was middle aged, starting to go bald but had a nice thick mustache and beard.

"Oh. Okay. Well, I guess I don't need anything. On second thought, do you have a picture frame?"

"Yes, several." He walked out from behind the counter and Lou followed him to a shelf on the back wall. "This five by seven with a glass is nice."

"Yes, I think that will work. How much is it?"

"A quarter of a dollar." He took the frame and went to the register.

"You don't happen to have a couple silver dollars and a two dollar bill in the register?" Lou followed him to the counter.

"Let me look." The register made a high pitch sound as he opened the cash drawer. "Yes, I do have both."

Lou handed him a five dollar note, "Great. Do you have an ink pen that I could use?"

Ken Wilbur

"Yes, we have that too." He handed Lou a pen and a bottle of ink. "Here is your seventy-five cents change."

Lou opened the back of the frame, and on the paper that was in it he wrote, Martha on one side near the top and Jesse on the other side. Down near the bottom he wrote Mr. and Mrs. Collins. He placed one of the silver dollars under each name and the two dollar bill above the couple's new name. He closed up the back of the frame and turned it to look at the finished work. He hoped they would think of it as two singles coming together to make a couple.

"Thanks, think this will do just fine." Lou handed him the pen and ink and turned to leave. He put the frame in his saddle bag and mounted Lucky.

As he rode past the railway station he wondered if it wouldn't be better if he caught the north bound train to Cheyenne and took the Union Pacific west to California without stopping at the valley. He wanted to see the people in the valley but he didn't want to spoil Squirt's wedding day.

Lucky seemed to make up his mind for him as he turned northwest toward the valley. Lou's mind was racing with all sorts of bad occurrences that could take place. He didn't want the final outcome of his visit to be bad or spoil the day for anyone.

His mood had changed. He was so happy and positive as he rode into Bear Lake and now he was depressed, worried that regardless of what he did, it would be wrong. Everyone was bound to find out that he had been in Bear Lake. If he did not go to the valley they would be upset with him but if he did and he spoiled the wedding that would be even worse. Why did life have to be so complicated? His decision would affect more than just himself.

While he was mulling this over in his mind, Lucky was eating up the miles to the valley. When he came to the gate with the big sign hanging over it, Lucky's head and ears perked up. He now knew for sure where he was and where they were going. Lou got down to open the gate and Lucky pawed the ground, anxious and eager to race to the barn.

They passed cows with young caves and mares with young foals, this was the time of year when it was fun to ride among the mares to

124

see the characteristics of their efforts. Lou could see Blue Eagle is some of the young colts. Blue Eagle showed up in the fillies also but it seemed more subdued. Watching the young offspring Lou forgot for a moment where he was going and what was waiting for him. Lucky had picked up the pace and Lou had to hold on to his Fedora so that it didn't fly off his head.

Lucky slid to a stop at the hitch rail between Wade and Sweeny's cabins. Lou could see all the buckboards and buggies at the church. He dismounted and using his hand he did his best to knock out some of the trail dust from his coat and pants. He started to walk toward the church when he saw Squirt. She was wearing the white satin dress Mrs. Collin's had made for her. She acted as if she expected him to ride up and was waiting for him. Lou could see a slight smile, the smile he had seen so many times before when she would beat him at a game of checkers or a card game.

She walked up to him and gave him a hug. She reached up and took off his fedora and put it in a buggy. Using her fingers she combed his hair. Lou was at a loss for words. She took his arm and turned to walk toward the church door.

"Whoa. I can't walk in with you." She gave him a tug but it was if his feet were nailed to the ground.

"Sure you can, they are waiting for us."

"What do you mean they are waiting for us, waiting for us to do what?"

"They are waiting for us to come in and get married." Again the little smile as if she had just won the game.

"What?"

"I told them I couldn't let you go to California alone, that without me you would just get into more trouble. You see what has happened this past year. Grandpa Schroeder said we had to be married if I were to go with you. Mom and dad agreed with him. So I said fine, we would get married." She gave a tug but his feet still would not move.

"I don't get any say in this? I thought you and Jesse were getting married. What happened to that?" Lou was puzzled, confused to say the least.

"Jesse is a fine young man and any gal would be lucky to have him. But he doesn't need me like you do and I don't feel for him like I do for you. Yes, you have a say in this. It takes two to get married, do you want to get married?"

"Well, Yes. But I thought I had to ask you and go to your father and ask him for your hand or something like that."

"Well, these are different times. I thought it called for a different solution. Should we go get hitched or stand here and talk about it? If we get married we have all the way to California to talk about it." This time the tug on his arm moved his feet toward the church door. Lou was in a state of shock, he was confused. He had thought about putting up a fight for Squirt but he wanted her to be happy and he thought she was happy with Jesse. He had made a mess of things and deep down he felt she deserved better then what he had to offer. He had planned to come back to the valley and spend a few days and see if he could win her away from Jesse. When the man in Bear Lake told him she was at the valley getting married he thought he had missed his chance.

With the opening of the church door, Sarah began playing the Wedding March on the church organ and everyone in the church came to their feet. *

Lou and Martha, arm in arm walked, slowly down the aisle toward the podium where Jokob waited. Standing on each side of the podium were Dusty and Sarah.

*Felix Mendelssohn wrote the Wedding March in C major in 1842

The small church was packed with family. Kemp and Pat in the first pew on the right and Wade and Judith on the left. Lou's little sister was standing by the organ waiting to sing.

"Dearly beloved, we are gathered here today to join these two young Christians in Holy wedlock." Martha squeezed Lou's arm and looked up to see a stunned look on his face. She had to restrain a giggle. Poor Lou, this is supposed to be the happiest day of his life and he looks like he is about to be sick.

Lou heard Jokob's words and he felt a drop of fear in his belly. His next thought was, "Wait a minute. I am not supposed to be scared, I am living out the dream I had last night." He took a deep breath and looked down at the smiling face of Squirt and he relaxed.

Lou's little sister stepped out as Sarah played the introduction to, I Leave My Heart with Thee*

"The fragrant wreaths my eyes invite, thy beauties smile around
In roses red, in roses white, thy blooming sweets are found.
No others charm my mem' can cheer alike all seem to me,
For ah, my love, my only dear I leave my heart with thee."

Caroline sang with the voice of a young angel. Her soprano voice sounded accomplished and sweet. Even if it was not quite the voice of an angel, it came close and it gave Luta chills. Luta thought how adorable and talented his little sister was and how proud of her he was.

Jokob's deep baritone voice resounded throughout the small church. "Who gives this bride in marriage?"

"I and her mother." Wade's voice seemed a little higher than usual, this was his baby girl and unlike Chet and Sarah she would not be living near them.

"Luta Schroeder wilt thou have Martha Wilbur to be thy wedded wife to live together in God's ordinance in the Holy Estate of Matrimony? Wilt thou love her, comfort her, honor and keep her as long as ye both shall live?"

"I will." Luta was no longer anxious or uncertain.

"Martha Wilbur wilt thou have Luta Schroeder to be thy wedded husband to live together in God's ordinance in the Holy Estate of Matrimony? Wilt thou love him, comfort him, honor and keep him as long as ye both shall live?"

"I will."

*Lyrics are unknown, music was written by James Hook in 1804

"Luta and Martha, you enter into this marriage knowing that the magic of love is not to avoid changes, but to navigate them successfully until death parts you. By the grace of God I now pronounce you husband and wife. Luta you may kiss your bride."

Sarah played as loud as the organ would allow and everyone clapped and cheered as Luta kissed his bride. Truth be told, it was more Squirt pulling Lou down to her lips as she was on her tip toes.

They had a feast of ham, venison roast, and of course beef. An abundance of sumptuous pies and cakes. Lou and Martha were too busy talking with family and excited to eat much. They did have to cut and eat some of the wedding cake that Judith made, again to the cheers of family.

They kept asking Lou questions and he did not know the answers. When are you leaving for California? Where in California are you going? What will you be doing? He didn't even know where they were going to spend the night, say nothing of what he would do in California. When it was just him he didn't need any plans but now that they were married it was different. He couldn't ask Squirt to rough it in a mining camp or room in a fleabag rundown hotel while they made a decision what to invest their money in.

Things changed so fast, Chet was a father and a very proud father. Carlos was the main attraction. He was passed from person to person, even his great grandfather Jokob had to have his turn. When Chet held him out to Luta it brought back memories of holding his little sister. Little Carlos grabbed Luta's nose and twisted it as if it were a knob. He was fine until he spotted his mother and then he wanted her. He held out his arms to Carmen and gave a squeal.

CHAPTER THIRTY-TWO

"So what about this money? You don't feel any remorse about spending it?" Lou and Squirt's parents were with them at the table talking about their future and Lou's mother asked the question they all had all been wanting an answer to.

"I know that I should but I don't. I feel if it were not for the railroad, the girls wouldn't be on that reservation. Without the railroad, I don't know if I would have grown up in a Cheyenne village, but I do think life on these plains would be very different. Without the railroad we would have buffalo roaming the plains and with buffalo the Indian tribes could survive. I don't know if it's just my mind tricking me into thinking it is okay for me to spend the money or if Satan is doing his work. I don't feel like the railroad or anyone owes me anything. In fact I feel like I owe you." Lou took a sip of his coffee.

"The money may not have been the most valuable thing you took from that mail car." They all looked to Wade, waiting for him to explain his statement.

"You also took the books that changed three lives, and you also took the knowledge that you did not want to be an outlaw. Those two things are the main reason we are here today at this table."

"I don't know if it is Satan or the Lord telling me that it depends on what we do with the money that counts the most. So far the money for the girls, the Library, seems to me to have been put to good use." Martha put her hand on Lou's arm and gave him a little wink.

"You're not saying it is okay to steal if you use the money in a good way are you?" Judith got up from the table and went to the stove to get the coffee pot. "I know what your grandfather would say."

"That is true Sis, but father did change greatly from St. Joe to Denver. I remember him being very upset with Wade for not allowing those renegades to come into camp. He said all they wanted was a hot cup of coffee. But when they opened fire on us and had us in a bad way, and Spotted Tail and his braves saved our bacon, father didn't say anything about the Indians taking scalps and striping the renegades of anything of value. In fact as I recall he got us all together and thanked the Lord. As I have heard him say many times, the Lord works in strange ways." Kemp held out his cup so his sister could refill it.

"I have said many times in my life that I could not change what had been done and at times I wanted to give up but I am pleased that I did what I had to do and that life has worked out like it has." Pat put her hand over her cup to show Judith that she had enough.

"I can't say too much, I stole Blue Eagle from that Yankee garrison."

"Yes, and I do remember telling you that we had to hide Dull Knife and lie to the Cavalry." Judith stood holding the coffee pot looking out the window as if she could see the band of Cherokee they had helped escape the Cavalry.

"What do you think you would like to do in California?" Wade held his cup out to Judith.

"Well, I think horses is what we both know the best, horses and cattle."

"You don't think you would like to continue to be a lawyer, you play the part so well?" Squirt could not help the giggle that followed her question.

"I think I will quite being a lawyer and an outlaw while I am ahead. I am not proud of what I have done, I would like to be proud of what I do in the future."

"Well, if you are thinking about raising horses, I would suggest that you take a couple of the mares that have not foaled and a young stud horse. The cost of freight will be much less than their cost to buy them out there. Plus, you will have this blood line." Wade was very proud of the blood line they had developed.

"I hate to think of leaving Lucky. I have had him at my side since the day he was weaned."

They all heard the loud knock on the door, but before they could do anything Sweeny and Penny walked in. "Got any hot coffee and words of wisdom left?" As usual, Sweeny had a big grin on his face.

"Why don't we ladies go into the living room and leave the men here at the table." Judith said as she got up and Sweeny took her chair and the cup of coffee she got for him.

"I was just telling Luta that if he and Martha plan to go into the horse business they should take a couple mares and a young stud. I think the freight will be far less than buying some good stock in California. What do you think?" Wade took a sip of his cold coffee, made a face and pushed it away from him.

"I agree. They could take a couple of those late mares and be way ahead of the game." Sweeny sipped on his coffee. "If they get out there and for some reason decide not to raise horses, the mares, foals and young stud would be like money in the bank."

"Think I could take Lucky and a young stud in the same rail car with the mares?"

"I think so. If you put the mares between them. Lucky won't cause any trouble and we got that one young stud that looks just like Blue Eagle that is real calm. You know the one I'm talking about, Wade?"

"Yeah, and I agree. Have you and Martha talked about when you will be leaving?"

"No, we talked about going to see Grandpa and Grandma and she would also like to go say goodbye to the Collins. I am guessing it will be a couple days, if not longer."

It was later, in the barn, when Lou and Squirt were finally alone. They had come out to get his dirty clothes out of his saddle bags. "So, just how surprised were you?" Martha was unbuckling his saddle bag. "When we got to the door of the church I thought you were going to be sick."

"Oh, you didn't surprise me. I rather expected something like that to happen." Lou said in a matter-of-fact way.

She reached into his saddle bag and felt the picture frame. She took it out and looked at it. "Oh, and why did you make this?" She held it up with a grin from ear to ear. Lou had forgot all about his gift. His nonchalant manner changed, but he didn't have a good answer.

"This is just one of the things that I love about you. You were thinking of me and you made a gift that you thought I would like. Well, I do like it and we will take it apart, cross out Jesse, put in Lou, and keep it on our bedroom wall forever." She went to him and gave him a hug and kiss.

"But how did you know I was coming? What if I hadn't shown up for a couple days?"

"The man at the store sent his son to tell us that you were in Bear Lake and would be coming to the valley. That gave us enough time to spread the word and get everyone to the church. I had talked with gramps, told him I had made a decision. We went over the wedding vows, so that we would be ready when you got here."

"Speaking of the wedding vows, what happened to, 'I Obey'?"

"Gramps and I talked about that and I told him that if it was not in your part that I would not agree to it in my part. He said that it was traditional for the woman to say it but not the man. I said not this woman, so he thought it best just to leave it out." She was standing looking up at Lou with her hands locked behind his head.

"What else did you and gramps talk about?"

"Gramps said marriage is like a river flowing past. You cannot touch the same water twice. You put your hand in the river, take it out, put it in again, and the water you just touched has gone down stream. He said this means that whatever you do in a marriage happens only once and then it is gone."

"Interesting. Gramps is a wise man. How did you make your decision?"

"Well, I knew I made the right decision because when I flipped a coin and while the coin, was in mid-air, I was hoping and praying that it was a head. I had said heads it was Lou and tails it was Jesse."

"What if it had been tails?"

"It was tails, so I went two out of three." She giggled as she told him

EPILOGUE

Beni and Aamu were very successful with their school and Library. In 1890 when Wyoming became a state they helped many of their tribe to get homesteads. Each plot covered a quarter of a square mile. Later they used the stories of the elders published in their newspaper to write a book. It was years later that they got a visit from Lou and Martha.

Lou and Martha had an exciting journey. California experienced an economic boom that they were a part of. Stockton was where they made their home. It was one of the richest agricultural regions and dairy legions in California. The climate was warm, sunny and a vast array of agricultural products thrived there. Wines were produced from vineyards north of Stockton which contributed to its economy. Lou and Martha were involved in everything from the local school board to state politics.

OTHER WORKS BY KEN WILBUR

Blue Eagle the story of a young Confederate soldier at the end of the Civil War and his black stallion, Blue Eagle.

Eagle Brand the story of three young Colorado men going to Texas and finding more than they bargained for.

Eagle Valley the story of how Native Americans and White settlers could live together in peace to the point of helping each other to survive.

Eagle Flight the story of a young baseball player from the little town of Randalia, Iowa going to Chicago to play for the Chicago White Stocking and the story of a young nun leaving the convent to find out who murdered her father.

+K

Rex Wilbur

Printed in the United States
By Bookmasters